A DIFFERENT KIND OF LOVE- MYA & PHARAOH'S STORY

LEONNA RUCKER

Chapter One

PHARAOH

Sweat dripped from my face as I dribbled up the court. Looking around to see who I could pass it to, I saw one of the niggas on my team cut to the basket. I no-look passed it to him and he caught it and went up for a layup, missing it. This was the third time he messed up. I was never the one to care about these pickup games, but I had money on the line and I didn't like to lose. These were the courts me and my boys have been playing at for years and I never saw him playing ball here before today. Already, I knew he was out of place and in unfamiliar territory.

"Fuck! Somebody get this nigga off my court!" I yelled out looking for anybody else who wanted to play.

"Get em outta here coach!" My homeboy Mitch since pre-k, yelled out causing everybody on the court to laugh out.

Mitch was the calmer one out of the two of us. Even

though he did his dirt, he never let nobody see him sweat. In some situations he was the more rational one between me and him. I went to him before I did anything and vise versa. Mitch leaned on my family because he really never knew his. From what I knew, he never knew his dad, and his mom took him to his cousins house one day and never came back to get him.

Out here in Cali playing ball on the courts was our home away from home ever since we were kids. Playing ball was a way I could relieve stress from school and everything that I had going on at the time. I played up until the middle of my senior year in high school. Multiple colleges wanted to offer me full athletic scholarships, but I got locked up for felonious assault and I went on trial for murder. That ruined my chances. I could have been something with how good I played ball, but the streets made me and I was making too much money to stop. My mom never wanted the environment I grew up in to affect my life, but it did just that.

My mom is a strong Mexican queen. She used to be a social worker who helped kids who were having problems at home live a better life. She made it her mission to teach me Spanish along with English when I was growing up, so that I wouldn't have problems traveling back and forth. Growing up we bounced back between here and Mexico because my dad wanted us to live a good life. My mom had told me that since my dad was black, her parents didn't like the fact that they were together and had a baby out of wedlock. Shortly after they had me, they were married and moved to California. To this day we still visit Mexico to see my other side of the family.

"Nigga pass the ball right and maybe I can make it." He shot back making the whole court grow silent.

I looked over at him confused. I wasn't expecting him to say anything to me when I didn't ask for him to say shit back. I guess he didn't know me. He was definitely about to find out.

"Yo get this nigga off my fucking court before I lay his bitch ass out." I snarled walking up to him.

"Ay, maybe you should get on up out of here." Mitch spoke walking up between us trying to dead the situation before things got worse.

"Man watch out. Last time I checked this was a public court so I can stay." He pushed Mitch off of him and walked closer .

I knew Mitch wanted to say something back to him, but instead he took a step back to let me handle it.

"See that's where you are wrong. This is my court. My street, my block. Basically everything from West End to the Grove is mine, so like I said get the fuck off my court before you get carried off." I took my gun from the waistband of my shorts and pointed it at him making him jump a little.

People might wonder how I can play ball and keep my gun tucked. It wasn't as hard as it looked. The nigga looked at me and then around at everybody else on the court who stood behind me waiting for his reaction. Instead of moving he just looked at me.

"*¡Sal de aquí (Get out of here)!*" I yelled and pointed off the courts.

Once he was off the court I chuckled and tucked my gun back into my waistband.

"Alright let's start over three on three first to ten. Y'all got runs y'all need to get done." I shook my head and grabbed the ball off the ground.

Even if he wanted to pop off, he wouldn't have gotten far because everybody on the courts worked for me. He made the right choice to run off before things got crazy.

———

"*Y*'all gotta be better than that. How y'all let us come back when we were down seven to zero." I yelled out wiping my face with my shirt.

"Man Nate kept missing shit." Mitch sat down on the bleachers and leaned back.

"Nah nigga don't blame that shit on me, you just stopped checking up on Ro. That's how he shot all of them three's out of nowhere." Nate shot back.

"He wasn't checking up on me before. I just let y'all think y'all had a chance. I told y'all I need to earn my money. I can't win it too easily." I chuckled and ran my hand through my damp curls.

"Y'all pulling up to the party tonight on Tiffin?" Nate asked.

Before either of us could respond gunshots rang out.

Mitch got hit in the shoulder right beside me and instead of getting down like the rest of the niggas on the court, I took my gun out of my waistband. Ducking, I looked around trying to figure out where the gunshots were coming from, and saw a nigga sticking out the sunroof with AK-47. Aiming my 9 mil in the direction of the moving car, I started shooting back. Dogs were barking and sirens were blaring in the distance after the shooting stopped and the car sped off down the street.

Running over to Mitch I bent down to see where he was hit exactly.

"¿Estás bien mano (Are you good bro)?" I asked, making sure he was okay as I looked him over.

Mitch was black, but since he was around me for so long he picked up on my Spanish. Going back and forth between Spanish and English was normal to me.

"Yeah man I'm straight. Fuck! This shit hurt like fuck." He hissed pressing down on his bleeding shoulder.

"Nate go get my car. Go! We gotta get you to the hospital." I spoke picking up both of our gym bags as Nate ran off.

"Nigga you not going to help me up?" Mitch asked, making me look over at him confused.

"Mano he ain't hit you in yo legs you can get yo ass up and walk." I sucked my teeth as we both laughed out before he hissed again.

Nate honked the horn of my car as the police sirens grew closer. Mitch and I ran to the car and I tossed our bags in the back seat before getting in the passenger side. Once we were all in the car, Nate sped out of the parking lot and to the hospital.

After three hours of them trying to get answers as to how Mitch got shot and then patching him up, it was time to go. I still had to figure out who did the drive-by today. As I thought about it I figured it couldn't be anybody but the niggas from the Valley because we had did a lick on them two weeks ago. This must have been them retaliating. I don't take kindly to getting shot at so they had to come harder than that. They were lucky Mitch was only shot in the shoulder because if he would have died I would have taken out their whole family tree. Since Mitch couldn't leave until they checked him out, I went to pick him up something to eat. He kept complaining about having to eat the hospital food.

Walking back into the hospital from BJ's Burger Joint, I looked down at my phone to see if Nate had heard anything about the drive-by. After reading his text that said the streets weren't talking, I sucked my teeth before I ran into something knocking the bag from BJ's Burger Joint out of my hand.

"Fuck!" I cursed as I bent down picking the bag up off of the floor.

"I'm so so sorry." Came from whoever I ran into causing me to look up at a girl who had bruises all over her face.

Picking the bag up off the floor, I stood up to get a better look at her. Even though she had a busted lip, a fat bruised cheek and stitches on her left eyebrow, she was still the most beautiful woman I've ever seen. She was small, about five-four.

Her dark brown hair was pulled up in a messy bun that sat at the top of her head. Her eyes are what sold me, they were like a greyish-hazel color and they drew me in. It was weird because she had on a turtle neck and a pair of baggy sweatpants that were too big to be hers. I must have been staring too hard because she tried to turn her face away so that I couldn't see it. Out of habit I reached out and touched her chin making her jump take a step back before rubbing her elbow nervously.

"It's all good ma. You good?" I asked, concerned.

"Yeah I'm okay you didn't run into me that hard." She chuckled and looked at me briefly before looking back down at the ground.

"Nah I meant are you okay?" I asked again, grabbing her chin and lifting her head up to look at me.

"Yeah yeah I'm okay I just fell down the stairs." She rushed out looking around nervously.

She must have seen something because she tensed up and moved my hand off her chin before stepping back.

"You sure?" I raised my eyebrow because I knew that falling down some stairs didn't make her face look like that.

"Yeah, maybe you should go." She looked over again and her eyes grew wide.

I followed her eyes and saw the nigga from earlier walk up to us. He looked between the both of us and chuckled before grabbing the girl's hand and pulling her closer to him.

"What's going on over here?" He questioned looking down at the girl.

"We ran into each other and-" She started before she was cut off.

"Did I ask you to speak?" He questioned making her bite her lip.

"Aye, relax. We were just having a friendly conversation." I spoke, making him look up at me.

"See this right here? This mine and she doesn't have friendly conversations. Don't you need to be checking up on yo boy? We got some sharp shooters where I be." He grinned cockily making me grimace and look at him.

I knew now who set up the drive-by and how the girl got the bruises on her face. It wasn't from her falling down a flight of stairs either.

Instead of saying anything to him I cocked back and swung on him with my free hand, splitting his lip instantly. We were in a hospital so I couldn't do him how I really wanted so This would have to work for now. Before I could hit him again one of the nurses walked up and asked if everything was okay. Ignoring her I stepped up to the nigga sized him up.

"Best believe I got shooters where I be, but mine take bodies with them. Keep yo eyes peeled *cabrón*," I looked at him briefly before looking down at the girl who looked at me.

"I will see you later beautiful," I winked at her and she looked down at the ground again.

With that I walked away and into Mitch's room. I most definitely was going to see her again.

Chapter Two

MYA

When we got into the house I knew Damien was going to be on bullshit because he hadn't uttered a word since we left the hospital. He just sat in the passenger seat holding onto his swollen lip. I didn't know exactly why the man at the hospital punched him, but I couldn't say that Damien didn't deserve it. He followed close behind me huffing angrily, all the way to our room.

"So that was yo nigga?" Damien asked, as he slammed the door to our bedroom making me jump.

"No Damien, I told you I don't know who that was." I stated honestly, as I sat on our bed and started taking off my shoes.

The man that bumped into me at the hospital was somebody I truly never seen before. He caught me off guard with how attractive and caring he was. We had never even met before today and it seemed he cared about me instantly. I never got a chance to ask him his name. This man was fine. He kept staring at me even when Damien walked up. I couldn't get caught looking at him because I knew Damien would get upset, I just couldn't help myself. He was tall and light-skinned and his eyes sparkled a light hazel. Damien had him a little on height, but the man had Damien beat on everything else. He had curly faded hair dyed brown at the tips. He had tattoos that covered his arms from what I saw in the wife beater he wore. I only saw it briefly after he punched Damien, but his smile was everything. I could tell he was a little jacked by the way his arms were set up in his wife beater.

Before I could finish, Damien rushed over to me and grabbed me by my chin making me look up at him. Damien was tall and lanky, always been, but he was solid. He was light skinned with sandy brown hair and blue eyes the color of the sky. The saying was right, evil people did have the prettiest face.

"You look at me when you speak to me." He snarled at me as I looked up him. "Let me find out you out here giving my pussy away I will fucking kill you. Do you hear me?" He yelled.

"Yes." I answered simply.

"Good, go get your ass in the shower. I'm about to go out and handle some business. Stay yo little ass in the house and don't let me get back and you're gone." With that he let go of my chin and turned around, walking out of our room and closing the door behind him.

Standing there for a couple minutes, I made sure he was leaving and then I started walking around. How was I supposed to go anywhere when he took my car that I bought with the money that I earned working for one of the best female defense attorney's there was in California. I was her assistant and she taught me the in's and out's about everything I needed to know about being a defense attorney. I passed my bar exam so all that was left was for me to get an actual case. I was going to be just like her when I finally got a case .

Walking into the bathroom, I looked at myself in the mirror and ran my hand across the stitches that ran across my eyebrow. Trailing my hand down my face to the bruise on my cheek that was turning blue and purple. Knowing I would have to cake myself in makeup to cover it completely, I pouted. Taking my bottom lip into my mouth and tasted the blood that had dried up on it. Dropping my head, I turned on the faucet to the sink. Grabbing my rag, I wet it, and then started dabbing my face lightly.

This wasn't the first time Damien had hit me. People would ask me why I was still with him even though he hit me when he got mad at me. I would always tell them that he does it because he loves me. I knew deep down that he was a good man. He didn't always hit me. We have been together for five years. High school sweethearts. He didn't start hitting me until we moved in together after college. We decided to go to different schools after high school. I chose to go to Stanford and he went to UCLA to play basketball. After blowing both of his knees out, he was dropped from the team and then he dropped out of college.

After a couple of months of him being out of college we started arguing a lot more and then the hitting started. I thought it would stop and we would get back to how we were, but it was starting to get old. I was tired of trying to make it work. Damien has to change or I am going to leave.

The doorbell rang scaring me out of my thoughts. Thinking it was Damien forgetting something, I rushed down the stairs and opened the door. I dropped my head when I saw my two bestfriends standing outside dressed like they were getting ready to go out. Aliyah had on a black leather mini dress with red high heels. Kris had on a pair of blue skinny jeans and patchwork jean jacket, and a pair of blue and white balenciaga's,

"Eww hoe what the fuck happened to your face?" My friend Kris questioned scrunching his face up at me.

"Nothing I ran into the door. What are y'all doing here?" I stepped back letting them in.

"We came to see if you wanted to go out tonight. Are you sure you didn't get hit with something more alive?" My other friend Aaliyah questioned looking at me suspiciously.

We rarely hung out when Damien would leave visible bruises because I didn't want them judging me and asking so many questions.

"Yes I'm sure. I can't go anywhere tonight so you guys can

go without me. I have a lot of work to do," I lied, walking up the stairs to my room.

"Oh hell no. You didn't come out last week or the two weeks before that. Your work is not that serious that you can't take a night off, so I'm going to need you to put on something sexy and let's go." Kris pushed his way up the stairs and went straight to my closet.

Sitting on my bed, I gently ran my hands down my face as Aaliyah came and sat next to me. I looked over at her and she put her hand on my shoulder.

"You know you can talk to us right?" She questioned.

Aaliyah and I first met back in the third grade when we saw each other at the playground. She was like a sister to me. We were joined at the hip, practically inseparable. We didn't meet Kris until our senior year in high school when he moved to town. He played basketball up until he graduated, he loved it and would always find his way near a group of men. People didn't really like him though because he was blunt and outspoken. That didn't take away from the fact that he was one of the realest people I have ever met.

"I'm okay I promise." I responded not looking at her.

Instead I looked at Kris who raided my closet without a care in the world. My closet was huge and I had a lot of clothes, even though I barely got to go anywhere besides work. Kris stayed trying to dress me up, but I could never complain because he never let me go anywhere with him, looking crazy.

"Okay so go ahead and put this on with these nude heels

you got. Hurry up because I still have to beat your face and time is running out." Kris spoke, walking over to me and laying the little outfit across my lap.

I looked down at the tight nude mini skirt and bralet set and sighed knowing Damien would have a fit if he caught me coming home in this. Especially if he told me not to leave the house anyway. I was going to text him and let him know that I was spending the night over Aaliyah house to clear my head. After a quick thought I stood up and started walking to the bathroom, before I turned around and looked at Aaliyah.

"Can I spend the night tonight?" I questioned.

"Yeah you know you can."

"Are we having a girls night tonight?" Kris asked, jumping into the conversation.

"Yes girls night as in me and Mya." Aaliyah chuckled as she sat crisscross on my bed.

"See y'all not even right. Don't even play with me like that." Kris whined

"I'm just playing with your crybaby ass, but just know your snoring ass will be sleeping on the couch." Aaliyah stated matter of factly.

"Whatever hoe, I don't snore for your information."

"Yes the fuck you do." I interjected.

"Hoe go get dressed so we can go." Kris spoke, blowing me off.

"I am. Can y'all pack me an overnight bag? My duffle bag in the closet and make sure y'all pack my laptop." I stated rushing to the bathroom

"Yeah yeah hurry up." Kris waved me off and made his way back over to my closet.

Rolling my eyes, I chuckled before walking into the bathroom. As soon as the door closed behind me, the smile on my face disappeared. I turned on the shower and stripped out of my clothes. Making sure the water was steaming hot out I stepped into it and let the hot water run over me. Stepping closer to the water so that I was under the faucet I took my time touching my bruises. I ran my hands over the week-old bruises that covered my torso. Some of them were still sore and then some were finally getting lighter and going away.

After about thirty minutes there was banging on the door breaking me out of my sorrowful thoughts. Turning the shower off and stepping out, I asked whoever it was on the other side what they wanted.

"Hoe when I said hurry up I meant just that. I didn't get all cute and shit to sit in the house and miss the party so chop chop before we leave your ass." Kris yelled from the other side of the door making me laugh.

He always wanted to be the dramatic extra one when we all knew that he took the longest to get dressed. Instead of answering him I dried myself off and put on my clothes. Walking up to the mirror I brushed my hair into a tight bun. I made sure that it looked good before I stepped out of the bathroom. As soon as I stepped out of the bathroom, Kris started screaming and clapping.

"Yes bitch, that's more like it. Now come and sit down so I can beat your face and hide what the *door* did to you." He emphasized the door because he knew that a door didn't do it.

Rolling my eyes I sat down on my bed as Kris went to work on my face.

Chapter Three

PHARAOH

"*Keep me a check, I ain't got no regrets. If I said it I motherfuckin' mean it. I'm a big dawg, a lieutenant.*" *Lil Baby's* hit single *Minute* blasted from the mansion party speakers as I looked around from the balcony. One thing I hated about parties is that they never seemed to have the air on, so the more people that came in the more I started to sweat. This mansion was big as fuck, but it had to be at least five hundred people here.

"Aye Dakota, where are all the bottles at?" I questioned looking back at my niggas who stood in the hallway talking with each other.

"They are in the kitchen and make sure you get some wraps from behind the bar so we can gas this bitch up." He replied over the music as he continued to watch the girl twerking in front of him try to keep up with the song.

Laughing and walking down the stairs to the kitchen, I needed to get a couple drinks in me so I could enjoy myself tonight. Walking into the kitchen I heard somebody talking real loud about how they were going to get somebody jumped. How many people were in the kitchen or who they were talking to because I was so focused on my phone. When the talking stopped and the room got quiet I looked up from my phone to see two females and a nigga looking at me. Putting my phone in my pocket, I looked around at all of them until my eyes fell on the girl I saw earlier at the hospital.

She looked a lot better from when I saw her at the hospital earlier. She was even more beautiful. The nude two piece set she had on made a nigga dick hard by just looking at her. I could see how nice her titties sat in the bralet she had on. A nigga ain't really care about her body too much though. Her face was all I kept focusing on.

"See now y'all that's what you call a fine man, hey daddy?" The nigga said catching me off guard.

"Aye! Chill out with all that shit. I don't get down like that." I stated sternly cutting my eyes at him.

"Oop, okay lil mexico. Y'all heard that sexy ass accent he just came in here with. Made me a little hot. Say something else." The nigga spoke back.

"What the fuck did I just say?" I asked, getting a little loud.

"My bad lil mexico." He apologized and smirked at me.

Instead of saying anything else, I turned my attention to the girl I saw earlier at the hospital. No matter how much makeup she tried to hide them behind, I could still see the bruising. We stared at each other for a few minutes before she broke eye contact and looked down at the ground.

Laughing to myself, I walked over to where the drinks were on the counter. It was still dead silent so I decided to say something.

"It's nice to see you again. How's your boy's lip?" I jokingly questioned as she looked up at me in surprise.

"Again? You know lil Mexico and you holding out on us?" The nigga asked putting his hand on his hip and looking back and forth between me and her.

"We met at the hospital earlier. Had a disagreement with her old boy. Nothing major." I looked at her as I answered his question.

She looked at me, but had yet to say a word. I could tell she wanted to though.

"So you're just going to keep looking at him and not say anything." The girl standing next to her said trying to get her to speak up.

She was cute too. She was taller than her friend standing next to her. She was the definition of a redbone. Had I seen her before I saw her friend I would have tried to shoot my shot with her. I was too focused on her friend to try now.

"*Mi error (My bad)* , I ain't mean to interrupt y'all. I just wanted to let you know that you look good tonight." I motioned to the girl from the hospital, as I poured me a cup of Patron and took a sip before I started to walk out of the kitchen.

"Wait hold on real quick Mexico! You really just going to let this nigga compliment you and walk away?" I heard the nigga yell out, making me stop and turn back around.

The girl from the hospital stood in the same spot still not saying anything, but her nigga friend walked up to me from behind the counter

"What's up?" I asked, as I took another sip of Patron.

"Im Kris, and those are my girls Aaliyah and Mya and we were wondering if we could come chill with you?" He asked, and I looked between the three of them.

"You sure about that? She ain't even said shit to me." I stated motioning toward the girl from the hospital.

"Yeah I'm sure. You just haven't asked her the right questions." He said as a matter of fact

"Alright, y'all can come chill whenever y'all ready we upstairs, but you have to calm down with all that gay shit." I took another sip of Patron and turned around.

Grabbing the wraps from the bar, I made my way back up the stairs. When I got up the stairs I tossed Dakota the wraps and told him to start rolling up. I was about to turn around and walk to the balcony when I felt a tap on my shoulder, so I turned to see the girl from the hospital and her friends. This time I took my time looking at how the nude mini skirt she had on hugged her thick thighs. Licking my lips, I drank the rest of my henny like it was a shot.

"Aye Ro what's up man who you over here-" Mitch walked over and threw his arm across my shoulder and stopped mid sentence once he saw who I was talking to.

"Hey I'm Aaliyah, and these are my friends Mya and Kris." Mya's friend spoke up answering Mitch's question.

"Aaliyah huh? Come mere let holla at you." He held his hand that was not in a sling out to Aaliyah friend and she quickly walked over to him.

After they walked away I turned my attention back to Mya. I had yet to take my eyes off of Mya as she looked around acting like she didn't notice me looking.

"Well I'm going to go look around for some snacks while y'all two stand here like y'all don't know how to talk." Mya's friend Kris said before shaking his head and walking away.

Laughing, I looked backed at Mya who was still nervously looking around with her arms crossed on her chest.

"So what's up *bebita*? Are you going to chill with me or what?"

"You speak fluent Spanish?" She asked not to acknowledge my questions.

"*¿Sí y tú?*" (Yes, and you) I asked, wondering if she understood me.

"No, but I did take a couple years of Spanish back in high school." She explained.

"Well maybe I can teach you a couple things." I smirked.

"I bet you can. So are we going to go sit down somewhere or are we going to stand here the whole time?" She smiled at me for the first time and I felt my heart melt.

She was really beautiful.

"We can sit down. Come on." I motioned her to me and

we walked over to a couple of chairs that were in the cut away from everybody.

Once we sat down I watched how soft and smooth her legs looked as she crossed them before catching me watching her.

"Why are you always looking at me?" She inquired.

"You're something nice to look at. It's only right for me to admire beauty when it's around." I smirked, making her smile back at me.

"You do know I have a boyfriend right?"

"Yeah I peeped, answer me this though Mya, how long have you been letting him hit on you?" I questioned making her look up at me in surprise.

"He doesn't hit on me, I told you I fell down the stairs." She tensed up and sat up in her seat nervously.

"You must think I'm retarted *bebita*. You're way too beautiful and to let him destroy it and then take up for him." I leaned back in my chair and looked at her.

I truly believed that every woman was like fine china. They were beautiful to look at but fragile to touch and easily broken. They were supposed to be put up to admire not ever to be laid a hand on. No matter how bad you wanted to lay a hand on them, you couldn't because it would be disrespectful. That's why I never condoned a nigga hitting his girl because he felt as though that was his way of showing her that he owned her. Niggas like Mya's boyfriend were pussies to me. Even though he acted hard, in real life he was scared. That's why he take his anger out on Mya, because he knew he would get beat the fuck up if he stepped to any other nigga on the street.Then it dawned on me. That's why he was so quick to go call his boys up earlier. He knew that they were way tougher than he was.

"He loves me." Was all she said in return.

I chuckled and shook my head. That's the oldest and most useless excuse in the book.

"If that's what you call love *bebita*, then I guess I don't know what it is."

Just then her phone started ringing. She quickly grabbed it out of her clutch and looked down at it. By the way she was looking I could tell she was scared to answer it.

"I'm guessing that's him calling now? You should answer that before he gets upset again." With that I stood up and started walking over to my boys who were passing blunts around like it was 4/20.

About fifteen minutes later I had smoked hella blunts and I was high as a motherfucker. I was vibing to the music with my eyes closed and another blunt in my hand when I heard my name being called. I opened my eyes and saw Mya standing in front of me.

"What's up *bebita*?" I looked up at her through hooded eyes as I took another hit from the blunt.

"Can I talk to you for a minute?" She asked nervously.

"For what? Where are your friends at?" I asked, not really in the mood to talk to her anymore.

"I don't know, that's why I wanted to talk to you."

I looked at her for a couple of seconds trying to decide if I should get up and talk to her or not. After a quick thought, I got up and walked out in front of her until I got to a quieter place.

"What did you want to talk about?"

"I want to know if you could give me a ride home?" She questioned hopeful.

"A ride home? You don't even know me. Where are your friends at?" I slightly raised my voice causing her to get tense.

"They are having fun and I didn't want to ruin it. I don't know anybody else here, but you and my house is over an hour away by bus because I don't have my car so can you please take me home? I have gas money if you want it." She smiled at me hoping that I would give in and I did just that.

"Come on man let's go. And I don't want your gas money." I chuckled and walked away from her, making my way out of the party.

$\mathcal{P}$ulling up to her house, I pulled up on the curb and turned the engine off before leaning back against my headrest and looking over at her. The whole ride to her house she was shaking and nervously looking out of the window. She didn't say much other than telling me how to get to her house.

"Thank you so much I appreciate it. How can I repay you?" She spoke so softly, her voice full of innocence.

"Take my number down and whenever you need me just give me a call." I stated honestly.

I looked over at her with seriousness written all over my face. She didn't have a response but she handed me her phone and I keyed my number in and saved it. Handing her phone back to her, I unlocked the door and she smiled and was about to step out. Before she could step all the way out I gently grabbed her wrist making her look back at me.

"Be safe and stay pretty, *bebita*. I mean what I said. Call my phone when you need me. " I winked at her and let her wrist go.

She understood what I said and she nodded her head before stepping out of the car and closing the door. I really hoped she understood what I was saying because I really needed her to stay safe and beautiful. There was no reason why all that should go to waste on a corny nigga. I waited until she opened the door to her house and then I started the car and sped off down the street.

Chapter Four

MYA

Walking into the house I closed the door and was about to walk up the stairs to my room when I heard something moving on the living room couch. I froze and my heart stopped as I heard footsteps coming towards me in the dark.

I was supposed to spend the night over Aaliyah house but when Damien called and told me that he needed me to come home, I left the party and came straight here.

The lights came on and Damien stood in front of me with anger written all over his face. He took a step back to look at what I had on, and then he snickered before he grabbed me by my neck. Raming me into the door he turned his lip up at me.

"Where the fuck were you at wearing this shit YaYa?" He spoke through gritted teeth as his grip on my neck got tighter.

I wanted to answer him but I couldn't breathe.

"Didn't I tell yo stupid ass to stay in the fucking house? You leave and then you have random niggas dropping you off and you thought I wouldn't fucking see you?"

"I...can't...breathe," Was the only thing I managed to get out before he let go.

Taking a huge breath of air, I rubbed my neck. I was pretty sure that because he was gripping my neck so tight there was a mark on it.

"You do stupid shit like this and you wonder why I get angry." He spoke a lot softer than he did before.

"I'm sorry. Aaliyah and Kris came over and they wanted me to come out since I wasn't able to see them last weekend." I confessed.

"So who the fuck just dropped you off then cause I know for a fact that wasn't Aaliyah car and Kris ain't got one."

"That was Kris's boyfriend he said he would drop me off." I lied

Hoping that he would believe me and end the conversation, but I was sadly mistaken when his face became twisted into a grimace again. He cocked back and punched me in my eye making me fall to the ground. I knew that I was going to have a black eye. That wasn't it, as I laid crying on the floor, he kicked and punched me a couple more times before he stopped and stood straight up.

"Do you think I'm fucking stupid bitch! When I tell yo ass to stay in the fucking house and don't leave I fucking mean it.

I don't give a fuck who came over to get you. Then you got random ass niggas dropping you off and lying about it like I didn't see who it was. That was the same nigga from the hospital earlier. So answer me this YaYa, if you don't know him why is he dropping you off? I dare you fucking lie to me again." He yelled in my face with rage in his voice.

At this point he was bent down so that he was eye level with me. Instead of saying anything, I dropped my head and cried. There was nothing I could say because I felt like nothing would make this situation better.

"That's what the fuck I thought, get your dumb ass off the fucking floor and don't let me see you in shit like that if it's not with me. Matter of fact when you take it off throw it in the garbage I don't want to see it again."

After he finished, he walked away and left me lying on the wooden floor. I laid there for what seemed like forever trying to regain vision in my right eye. When I finally made it to my room, Damien was fast asleep. I didn't feel right sleeping here with him like what just happened didn't so I called Aaliyah. When she didn't answer I called Kris but his phone went straight to voicemail. Sighing, I walked into the bathroom. Looking at myself in the mirror I could barely recognize myself. I reached up to touch my eye, but my body was sore from all the kicking and punching.

Slowly removing my skirt and bralet, and then I took off the makeup that covered my bruises. When I stood and looked at my body in the full length mirror I broke down crying. My life wasn't supposed to be like this. Damien and I were supposed to get married, and start a family. He was supposed to get into the NBA and I was supposed to be a lawyer. Damien changed and I believed that nothing could ever be the same anymore.

After I got out of the shower I tiptoed around the room as I put on my clothes. I was thinking about taking my car and going somewhere, but Damien had my keys. I thought for a second and then I remember that Ro had put his number in my phone. It was now two in the morning so I was hoping he would be up. I texted him instead of calling because I didn't want Damien to wake up even though he could sleep through almost anything, I didn't want to risk it.

Mya: Hey this is Mya, the girl you dropped off a while ago. I was wondering if I could take you up on your offer.

I started to walk back in the bathroom but before I could get there my phone started vibrating in my hand. Ro was calling me. I quickly walked in the bathroom and gently closed the door behind me before answering the phone.

"Hello?" I whispered in the phone quickly putting it to my ear.

"¿*Que pasa (What's up)*? Why are you whispering?" He spoke softly through the phone and his accent made my insides melt especially when he spoke Spanish.

"I need your help. Were you sleeping?" I whispered nervously.

"No, I'm riding around. What do you need help with?"

"I was wondering if you could come pick me up."

"Everything okay?"

"I'd rather tell you when you get here."

"Okay, I'll be there in five."

"Okay thank you."

"*No problema*."

I hung up the phone and smiled to myself before sliding my phone in my pocket and walking out of the bathroom. I quickly slid on my slides and walked out of the room. Finally making it outside I felt relieved. As soon as I walked down the driveway, Ro pulled up. I heard the locks on the car unlock and I quickly got in.

Instead of pulling off he locked the doors and looked at me. I tried to hide my face, but he turned my face towards him. He sat and looked at me for a long time before his facial expression changed. It was a mix between pity and anger.

"*¿Qué pasó (what happened) bebita?*" He questioned rubbing his goatee.

I realized that whenever he was upset or something he didn't like happened, Ro would always speak in Spanish. It was a good thing I knew basic Spanish because I would have been so confused.

"Can we go to your house?" I questioned not answering his question.

"Yeah if you are going to tell me everything when we get there." He answered calmly.

"I will."

"*Bein (Good)*." Was all he said before he pulled off down the street.

———

*T*hirty minutes went by and I started to realize where we were. I've heard a lot about this side of town. I just never decided to come this way. People were dying everyday, and if it wasn't by the police it was by the trigger happy people who thought shooting a gun would solve all of their problems. Ro must have sensed me tense up because he called my name making me look at him.

"You alright with me bebita, I'm not going to let anything happen to you while I'm around." He smiled at me and somehow I trusted every word he said.

A couple minutes later he pulled into the driveway of what I'm guessing was his house. His house wasn't big enough to be a mansion, but it was big enough to have a front gate. I noticed on the gate it had a beware of dog sign.

"You have dogs!" I asked in excitement as he pulled into the driveway.

"Yeah two red nose pitbulls." He smiled as he thought about them.

"Aww I love pitbulls."

"Have you ever had a dog before?"

"No but I've always wanted one."

"Well come on let me show you around."

He got out of the car and walked over to my side to let me out. Walking up the stairs to his house he unlocked the door. Before he opened the door he looked back at me and smiled.

"Brace yourself."

As soon as he opened the door and stepped in two huge brown pitbulls jumped on him. Their tails wagged as they licked him. They were excited to see him until they noticed me standing there. As soon as they laid their eyes on me they jumped off of him and started growling.

"*¡Silenció (Be quiet)!*" *Siéntate (Sit down)!*" When he yelled that, they both stopped growling and sat down.

They were still still staring at me and I felt like they would attack if I took a step.

"She's cool, y'all go chill in y'all room." He talked to them like they were human beings and they did just like he said.

After they were out of site he laughed and closed the door.

"How long have you had them?" I questioned because I had never seen dogs who obeyed like them.

"Since they were puppies. It took a while for them to get like they are, but it's worth it. Them my kids."

"That's so adorable."

"I guess, come on let me show you around."

Chapter Five

PHARAOH

"This is Chloe and Chaos' room right here." I spoke walking past it to get to the guest room where Mya would be sleeping.

I walked to the guest room and opened the door letting her in. She stepped into it and I turned on the light behind her. She looked around the room before walking over and sitting on the bed. I stood at the door and studied her with my arms crossed at my chest. When I noticed the handprint on her neck I grew angry.

"*¿Dónde más hay moretones (Where are the other bruises)?*" I asked about the bruises making her look up at me in confusion.

"What is *moretones?*" She questioned.

"Bruises."

"My eye is just black."

From the look on her face I knew she was lying.

"*Ven aquí.*" I responded telling her to come here.

She looked at me for a second before she got off the bed and slowly walked over to me. When she finally made it to me I reached my hand out to touch her, but she flinched and took a step back. It hurt my soul to see how scared she was.

"Come here, I'm not going to hurt you." I spoke calmly and she took a step forward.

When she was close enough I reached my hand out and ran my hand along the stitches on her eye, and then I gently touched the fresh black eye making her winch in pain. I ran my thumb over her busted lip and then the bruises on her cheek. I looked at the handprint on her neck closer and saw that it was red and purple.

"How long has he been hitting you Mya?"

"About two years now."

"You think that's what a nigga who loves you is suppose to do?"

"He loves me, we are just going through alot right now. It will get better, I know it will." She spoke up, taking up for him.

She sounded so unsure of herself. I just needed her to understand that's not how it's supposed to be. No matter how mad or how hard a nigga got, he was never supposed to hit a lady. That was the one thing my dad and all of my male family member's kept telling me.

"I want to show you something." I stuck out my hand for her to hold and when she did I stepped through the door and walked to the bathroom that was connected to the guest room. On the other side of the door there was a full length mirror. I pulled her inside of the bathroom with me and closed the door behind us.

"What are you doing?" She looked back at me confused and I turned her face back to the mirror never answering her question.

"Just bare with me *bebita*." I stated simply.

I needed her to see the problem. I knew there were more bruises that she wasn't telling me about, and I knew exactly where they hid. I slowly lifted her sweater up revealing bruise after bruise after bruise. I took it all the way off and tossed it on the floor before running my hands down every single last one of them. I stared at her through the mirror as she winced in pain at my touch for a second before she finally relaxed. I made sure not to leave one untouched as we looked each other dead in the eye. I wrapped my arms around her waist and held her close so that she could feel and hear every word that I was about to say.

"A nigga that really cares about you would hold you like this because he scared to let you go. A nigga that cares makes sure that nobody disrespects you not even him. A nigga that cares makes sure that you straight before anything. Most importantly a nigga that cares would never want to make you or even see you cry over something that he did."

I knew she had been listening to every word I said because her hands that were once on her side were now holding onto mine. At first I was just going to let her talk and then go into my room and call it a night, but when I saw all of the bruises he gave her I changed my mind. I started kissing her neck and she tensed up, but she never said no so I continued. I turned her body towards me as I kissed and licked every inch of the bruise on her neck. She put her hand on my shoulder making me look at her.

"You want me to stop?" I questioned hoping the answer would be no.

When she shook her head no I attacked her lips and picked her up, sitting her down on the bathroom counter. I quickly took her bra off and started sucking each one of her titties. After I finished showing each of them attention I started to kiss each of her bruises that covered her torso. I trailed my hands down her body making her shiver and then I gently picked her up and opened the bathroom door before I carried her to the room. Laying her on the bed I hovered over her as I openly admired how perfect her tittes sat up. I reached my hand up to the top of her leggings and slowly pulled them down along with her panties. When they were all the way off I trailed my index finger down the middle of her stomach. I didn't stop until I made it to her clit. I looked her dead in the eye as I inserted my middle and index finger inside making her moan out. She was already soaking wet so I moved my fingers in and out of her a couple of times before I took them out. I sucked my fingers off before I dipped my head down and tasted her sweet juices. I stayed down there for ten minutes before standing up and removed my shirt.

Mya looked at me in amazement and I removed my pants

and got on the bed. Mya licked her lips and scooted back on the bed. I smirked and crawled between her legs. Leaning down I latched my lips onto hers and I guided the tip of my dick at her entrance. I continued to kiss her as I slowly guided myself inside of her. She gasped against my lips and I started kissing her neck, making her grab ahold of me. Not long after, I was deep stroking her and looking her dead in her face. She screamed my name and took her bottom lip in her mouth. In one swift motion I pulled out and turned her around as I began to break her back in from behind. She screamed out louder and I smiled and grabbed a hold of her waist.

"You like this dick huh Mya?" I questioned.

"Yes." She answered before she started throwing it back on me.

"Throw that shit back then *bebita*."

I slapped her on the ass and she moaned out. I watched her throw it back on me in amazement. After letting her do her thing for a couple of minutes, I tried to take control once again but she had other plans. Before I could say or do anything she turned around and put me in her mouth. She looked up at me as she slowly tried to fit me all in her mouth. I smiled and caressed her cheek gently.

"Take it all in there and *bebita*, this is your dick now."

She listened and took it as far as it could go before she gagged and took it back out. She continued to do the same thing before she got used to it and started deep throating me faster.

"Fuck, yeah just like that." I grinded myself in and out of her mouth as she matched my pace.

She sucked me good for a couple of minutes before I pulled out of her mouth and bent down to kiss her. Our tongues wrestled with each other's as I ran my fingers through her hair. After a while I laid on my back and started to stroke myself as we looked at each other.

"This yo dick now right?" I questioned.

"I guess." She smiled and shrugged her shoulders.

"You guess? Well it is so how about you come ride it."

She smiled and crawled over to me as I pulled her on top of me. She slowly slid down on my dick and when she got used to it she started bouncing on it.

"There you go, ride yo dick then." I smiled up at her and put my hands behind my head.

She thought she was doing something until I started thrusting my hips upward and she started running.

"Oh my fucking God." She screamed out as she put her hands on my abs trying to hold me down.

"Move your hands and stop running from me Mya. God can't help you right now so take this dick." I smacked her on the ass before grabbing a hold of her waist holding her in place.

I continued to pound her shit in from the bottom making her scream out. I was going to show her exactly how a nigga who cared is supposed to treat that pussy tonight. I'm going fuck her like she was my wife tonight.

Chapter Six

MYA-1 MONTH LATER

"Well well well, it's nice for you to join us Mya." My boss said as I rushed into her office with her morning breakfast.

I sat her coffee down in front of her and then sat in the chair in front of her desk so that she could tell me what she needed to be done for today.

The bruises on my face had cleared up and me and Damien were doing fine. He apologized and he even took me to see my mom and dad in Southern California. They were so happy to see that we were still together. Damien tried to make it seem like he was the same person he had always been throughout high school, so I didn't mention that he had dropped out. They asked how Aaliyah and Kris were doing and I said they were great.

The whole time I was there I couldn't help but think

about Ro. I hadn't seen him since the night at his house. I haven't gotten a text or anything so I guessed it was a lost cause. I wasn't going to lie and say I felt bad about having sex with him because the whole night wrapped in his arms was amazing. It had been awhile since Damien had done anything like that.

"Sorry Jess, I got off the plane and came straight here. How are you on this beautiful Monday morning?" I questioned crossing my legs in the chair.

"I'm great thanks for asking. Let's get right to the point. I have a very notorious client who wants me to handle his case. He is currently in Twin Towers awaiting trial because the judge feels as though he is a flight risk. I'm going to go talk to him about his case in a half hour and I need you to come with me. You are going to be my secret weapon to win this case for him. Can you do that for me?" She asked, smiling at me.

"Yes I can do that." I spoke confidently.

"Great, I know you can I taught you well. While I eat this lovely breakfast you bought me, go ahead and read through his case file and think of some questions to ask so that we can get a better understanding of the charges. The file is on your desks, I'll be out shortly."

She smiled and I took that as my que and got up. I wasn't going to disappoint her, so I was going to try my best to make her happy.

———

*a*fter going through security, Jessica and I were escorted back to a private room in a separate part of the jail. When the guard unlocked the door and I walked in behind Jessica, my heart started beating fast. I had never stepped foot in a jail let alone talked to an actual inmate. I had to get over how nervous I was if I was going to do a good job for Jessica.

"Hi Pharaoh Rivera, I'm Jessica McDucan and this is Mya Sanders. You needed us to take your case for you?"

When he looked up at us in surprise my heart stopped. I had no idea that Ro was even in prison and now that I had read his file I was more shocked than he was. All this time he was in jail and I didn't even know it.

"That's cool since I had to fire my other one. Did my boy Mitch give you the money?" He questioned briefly looking at her before staring at me.

"Yes everything is taken care of," She nodded her head before her phone started ringing. "I have to take this, go ahead and get started with getting to know him, Mya. This will just take a minute." With that she walked out of the room.

I waited until the door closed before looking back at Pharaoh who smiled at me.

"Come sit down. Talk to me, how have you been?"

"Why haven't you called me?"

"I can't really do that if I'm in here can I?" He spoke sarcastically.

"I guess not." I answered sitting down.

He looked me dead in my eyes but I had no idea what to say to him. I didn't know how it would look to the grand jury if the defendant was talking to his defense attorney's assistant. I didn't want Damien to ever find out what happened between me and Pharaoh either. Ever since the night I had sex with Pharaoh, Damien has been back to his old self. The morning after when I came back home Damien was up making me breakfast. I made up a lie saying that Jessica had called me in for an early meeting. He had noticed that I was upset and didn't want to talk to him and he apologized and cried before telling me it wouldn't happen again. I told him that I forgave him, but if it happened again I was going to leave and never come back. Ever since then he hasn't even raised his voice again. I was happy to have my old Damien back again.

"So what's up *bebita*, how have you been? I missed you." Pharaoh reached his hand out and tried to touch mine, but I moved it out of his touch.

"I'm not here to talk about me right now, let's talk about you and why exactly are you here." I rebutted crossing my arms on my chest.

He looked at me for a second like he was thinking about something before he snickered and leaned back in his chair.

"I see you. You all about yo job huh?"

"Yes, I mean this is my job." I spoke sternly as he continued to smile at me.

"I like that, you really do have a backbone. I'm guessing

you and your nigga back on good terms, cause you acting like ain't shit happen between me and you the last time I saw you."

"I do have a backbone and nothing happened." I retorted simply making him laugh.

"I'm not even going to get into that with you in here. If you want to know, I got pulled over coming from your side of town. Corny ass cop pulled me over because he had never seen me over there before. I had rolled two blunts and was smoking one when he walked up so he told me to get out of the car. When I got out he decided to check my whole car and found three pounds of weed in a book bag in the passenger seat." He responded simply.

"And why did you have so much on you at one time?"

"For medical use. I got the license to prove it and everything. I just didn't have it on me at the time."

"And this policeman, he didn't have a warrant to search your car did he?" I asked, writing down what he had told me.

"Nah, not that I know of."

As soon as he finished his sentence, Jessica walked into the room. She looked between the both of us before she closed the door and walked up on the side of me.

"How's everything going in here? Mr. Rivera I have some good news for you." She smiled happily.

"Yeah everything is going good Mya here is really good at what she does. What's the good news?" He smirked at me and I could tell that there was a double meaning to what he was saying.

"I convinced the judge to let you out on bail saying that both your parents live here in California and you have to take care of them both. I already called your friend Mitch and he is on his way to post your bail. You should be out within the next hour. Don't let me down Mr. Rivera and I want to see you in my office tomorrow morning at nine o'clock sharp."

"Alright cool, make sure she's there too." He smiled at me.

Jessica looked at me and smiled as she put her hand in my shoulder. I smiled up at her before looking at Pharaoh. When he saw me looking his face had changed. Instead of the smile he had plastered on his face seconds before, he smirked at me. He knew exactly what he was doing.

"I will make sure of that. If you don't have anything else right now, you can talk to me in the morning. I mean it Mr. Rivera, nine o'clock sharp." She spoke sternly.

"I will be there. Which one of y'all do I call if I have anything else?"

"Uh, you can contact Mya, she is my assistant. She will share everything with me in the morning."

"Alright then I'll be seeing you two in the morning. Thank you again Ms. McDuncan. Ms. Sanders, I'll be in touch if I have any questions." He winked at me.

I stood up and walked to the door before turning around and looking at Pharaoh.

"Call me anytime you need me. I will see you tomorrow Mr. Rivera."

"You have a good day." He called out to me as I walked out of the door.

Chapter Seven

PHARAOH

I've only been gone a month and niggas out here acted like I was never getting out. As soon as I walked out from behind the jail walls and hopped in the passenger side of Mitch's Beamer, I was on a mission.

While I was locked up some niggas set my boy Nate up and got him killed. He was my transporter and they were trying to get information about where and how I got my shit. I'm guessing he ain't tell them shit because they killed him and everybody he was with. It's cool because I'm on their ass now.

"So what we got?" I loaded the extended clip of my *MPS* and looked over at Mitch whose eyes stayed focused on the road.

"We are about to hit a lick." He stated simply before taking a glance at me.

"I want everything so I need safe codes."

"Sayless."

"I want everything that moves dead!" I sneered, locking the clip into place and cocking it back.

"Bet." He nodded his head before making a sharp right into the parking garage.

We switched cars just in case somebody decided to follow us from the jail. I had to be careful because I didn't need any more chargers added onto the already fluke charges that they gave me. Mitch had told me that Jessica McDuncan was the best defense attorney in California, so after my old attorney couldn't even get me out on bail I dropped him and got in touch with Jessica. I didn't know that Mya worked for her. It was a good thing she was taking my case. Now I would be able to see her a little more.

We drove around for thirty minutes and then Mitch turned onto a street and stopped, turning the car off. I looked around and noticed that we were in the Valley so we must be where we needed to be.

"We here?" I questioned looking over at Mitch.

"Yeah it's the lime green house on the left." He responded as he loaded his 9mm.

"That's all you got *Mano?*" I chuckled looking at him like he was crazy.

"Nigga this all I need, let's go in here and get this over with. Always worried about what I got going on." He shot back as he got out of the car and started walking to the house.

I laughed and then followed behind him. Once we got the

door I knocked on it and put the hand that held the gun behind my back.

"Hold on a minute." A female voice came from behind the door.

We waited a couple seconds before the door opened. A lady stood at the door looking between Mitch and I. I looked at Mitch and nodded my head. He quickly grabbed her by the shirt and held the gun to her head, causing her to scream out.

"Shut yo stupid ass up." Mitch yelled, hitting her in the head with the barrel of the gun.

We rushed into the house and I closed the door behind us.

"Go ahead and get ole boy." I told her to look around for him.

"He is not here." She responded before I heard a loud thump on the floor above us.

"You fucking lying to me?" I questioned getting mad.

"No." She started whining so I knew she was lying.

I heard it again and I started shaking my head. It took everything in me not to kill her right now, but I wasn't going to quit yet I needed her as leverage.

"So who the fuck is that?" I grabbed a fistful of her hair and pulled her to me.

I told Mitch to walk up the stairs as me and the girl followed behind him. When we got all the way up the stairs, a nigga came walking out of the room with two duffle bags in his hands. He saw us standing there and took off running in the opposite direction. I wasn't about to chase him so I aimed and shot at his legs causing him to fall to the floor and dropped the duffel bags he was holding.

"Damn the party just started *Cabron,* where are you going? You see that man he was just going to leave you here, and you were being a good girl and trying to protect him." I ran my index finger down the side of her face making her squirm.

I passed the girl to Mitch who was standing close by, before walking up to the dude who was moaning in pain at the bullet holes in his legs. I bent down and unzipped both duffel bags.

"Oh you just made my day a whole lot easier. I appreciate you holding my shit for me *Cabron* I do, but what I do want to know is who else was with you when you took my shit and who y'all working for?" I asked zipping the bags up and putting them to the side.

"I don't know." He answered, simply making me shake my head.

"Y'all two some lying *hijos de puta (sons of bitches)*," I chuckled "*Mano* air her shit out." I told Mitch.

Just then he raised his gun and put two holes in her skull making her drop to the floor.

"Oh shit, okay okay. Tyrone, Big Dame, and Caesar . I hit the lick with Caesar but Tyrone and Big Dame set it up. Cameron told us where to go and who to hit." He blurred out looking between me, Mitch and the dead body on the floor.

"See *Cabron* now was that so hard?" I questioned picking up one of the duffle bags with my free hand.

He looked at me and shook his head.

"I know it wasn't," Was the last thing I said before I sent three shots to his body. "Grab that other bag and let's get up out of here." I told Mitch, turning around and walking down the stairs.

———

$\mathcal{W}$alking onto the porch, I dreaded knocking on the door ever since I found out what happened. Nate was my responsibility and I let him down. I wasn't even able to go see him at his funeral, so today I was going to pay my respects to his family. Clenching the duffle bag in my hand I knocked on the door and took a step back to wait. A couple seconds later I heard the locks being clicked. When the door opened I looked to see Nate's seven year old son staring up at me.

"Aww man what's up Uncle Ro." He smiled and ran up hugging my legs.

"What's up Tate, where yo mom and them at?" I questioned patting his back.

"They in the kitchen. Come on let me show you," He grabbed my hand and pulled me into the house, closing the door behind us. "Grandma, Mommy, Uncle Ro here!" He yelled out before we stepped into the kitchen.

When we made it to the kitchen Tate let go of my hand and ran over, sitting next to his grandma. I stood at the kitchen entrance to look around. There was mail everywhere and then I noticed the eviction notice sitting on the kitchen counter next to the trash. It instantly made me mad. I walked over and picked it up so I can't read it over. I knew when Nate died things were going to be hard, but I didn't know it was going to be like this.

"Y'all wasn't going to call me?" I questioned looking at Nate's mom and girlfriend for answers.

"We didn't know where you were, and the bills just kept piling up." His girlfriend responded from the stove.

"Well I'm here now, so look I got something for y'all." I walked over to the table and dropped the duffle bag onto it.

"What is this?" Nate's mother asked looking at the bag.

"Go ahead, look inside." I smiled looking at all of the curious faces.

Nate's mother unzipped the bag and looked inside before putting her hands to her mouth. A couple seconds later she started to cry causing Nate's girlfriend to walk over and look inside. She put her hands on her chest and looked over at me in awe. Inside the bag was half a mil, in all one hundred dollar bills.

"Omg Pharaoh, you didn't have to do this." His girlfriend said walking over and giving me a hug.

"Yes I did, Nate was like a brother to me and I should have been there to help him and I wasn't. Now I'm here to help y'all whenever y'all need me. I'm one phone call away. That's going to help y'all out a lot and if y'all ever need anything let me know. Y'all my family and family help, don't forget that." I spoke from the heart between the two of them.

"Thank you so much." She said walking back over to the

table and looking inside the bag just to make sure what she was seeing was real.

"Anytime y'all need me. I just came to drop that off to y'all, I'm about to head out. Come on Tate let me out." With that I turned around and started walking to the front door.

I heard Tate feet running up behind me and before I could make it all the way to the door, he hugged my legs from behind.

"Thank you Uncle Ro, I haven't seen them happy like that since my daddy died." He spoke looking up at me.

"You welcome Tate. Just know I'm going to make sure that y'all will never hurt again I promise." I turned around and hugged him back.

"Okay I'll see you later." He smiled before letting me out the door and closing it behind me.

Walking to my car I ran my hand down my face. I was going to kill every last person who had something to do with Nate dying, and I put that on everything.

Chapter Eight

MYA

"So we're just going to act like what happened between us never happened?" Pharaoh asked sitting across from me as I wrote notes down in my notepad.

"What happened?" I joked, quickly looking up at him.

"Man stop playing with me Mya, you know exactly what I'm talking about."

We were sitting at my desk getting his story together for his defense. Jessica was going to let me defend for her for the first time and I was working my hardest to make her proud. I had a feeling that my case was strong enough to win. Hopefully I do just that.

"Stop it Pharaoh. I have a boyfriend and now is really not the time for us to be talking about that." I spoke sternly and put my pen that I was writing with down so that he knew I wasn't playing.

"Why do you keep bringing him up like I care? If I cared about him and his feelings I wouldn't have done what I did to you. I know you still remember how I made you feel." He leaned onto the table and looked me dead in my eyes.

I would be lying if I told him that I didn't remember a thing. The way he made me feel that day was amazing. Damien was my first everything so all I knew was him. Pharaoh made me feel so good. He made me feel better than Damien ever did. He hit spots that Damien never did, but none of that mattered. I wasn't with Pharaoh, I was with Damien. I wasn't in love with Pharaoh, I was in love with Damien.

"It was wrong, none of that should have happened. It won't happen again." I spoke down to my notepad because I couldn't look him in the eyes.

"Right Right. Until you can look me in my eyes and tell me it was wrong and it won't happen again I won't believe you. In the meantime let's finish talking about this case." With that he leaned back in his chair and smiled at me.

I chuckled and shook my head as I picked up my pen to continue writing.

"So can we get to business?" I questioned seriously.

"Whenever you ready bebita." He responded shrugging his shoulders.

Just as I was about to start asking him more questions there was a knock on my office door and in walked the person I least expected to walk through the door.

Damien stood in my office with a bag of McDonald's in

his hands. At first he had one of the biggest smiles I had seen in a while plastered on his face and then when he saw Pharaoh his face changed. He was now sporting a mean mug and his hand that wasn't holding the food in it was bald into a fist.

"Hey baby what are you doing here?" I asked, getting up and walking up to him.

I tried to give him a kiss, but he turned away from me and looked at Pharaoh.

"What is he doing here YaYa?" He questioned slowly looking away from Pharaoh.

"We are working. What else does it look like *vato?*" Pharaoh answered, making me snap my head around and look at him.

"I wasn't talking to you." Damien looked down at me before looking back at Pharaoh.

It was something about the look in his eyes that made me nervous to even say anything else, so I just stood frozen looking up at him.

"You weren't, but I answered for her. Now if you don't mind I would like to finish working with my attorney." Pharaoh snapped back leaning on my desk.

"Can I talk to my girl in private?" Damien questioned as his jaw clenched.

"Go ahead. I'm not even here." Pharaoh joked as he looked up at Damien never cracking a smile.

"Pharaoh!" I snapped my head back deadlocking my eyes on his.

He slowly took his eyes off of Damien before looking at

me. He unbuttoned the jacket of his two piece suit and stood up. Walking to the door he never took his eyes off of me, but just before he opened the door he looked at Damien.

"I'll be right outside the door *bebita*." He opened the door and walked out, closing the door behind him.

I waited a couple of seconds before turning to Damien smiling as he looked back at me with disgust on his face. He took a couple steps back and locked the door to my office never once taking his eyes off of me.

"Before you say anything," I put my hands up trying to calm him down as he slowly walked up to me.

"I'm not calming the fuck down Mya. When I asked you who that pussy ass nigga was the first time you swore you ain't never seen him before. Now all of a sudden you got him dropping you off and you his attorney." Damien quickly yanked me up by the collar of my work shirt.

We were so close together that I could feel his heart beating against me.

"What is he giving you Mya huh? You give away my pussy Mya?" He sneered at me as he backed me into my desk.

"Damien I'm not giving him anything." I figured that he was going to hit me at any moment so I had my guards up.

"You lying to me Mya?"

"No-no I'm not." I held my hands against his chest to keep him from stepping any closer.

"So whose is it?" He quickly reached up my skirt and lifted me up onto my desk.

I kept my hands up until he moved my hands and stepped

forward. He pressed hard against me, all the while he started to finger me. I let out a moan and he latched his lips onto mine.

"Tell me whose pussy this is Mya." He spoke against my lips as he moved my thong to the side and inserted two fingers into me.

"It's yours." I spoke grinding at the same pace.

"I know it," He quickly unbuckled his belt and dropped his pants to the ground. "Come here." He pulled me to him and entered me without hesitation causing me to scream out in pain.

When I opened my eyes I saw him just looking at me. His eyes were so cold and there was no emotion in his face. I was scared by the way he was looking at me so I closed my eyes and hoped that it would be over soon. I caught myself thinking about the night me and Pharaoh had sex and started to believe he was the one I was having sex with. Pharaoh was much softer and slower at times. It felt like Damien just wanted to get it over with. I just imagined Pharaoh was ramming in and out of me. A couple of minutes later I cummed for Damien, something I hadn't done in a long while. Once I came I realized that Damien hadn't cum yet. He was still going faster and deeper. I sat there passionless as I kept my eyes closed.

"Shit Mya I'm about to cum." He cut me off guard when he pulled me closer and released his load into me.

We had agreed that we would have kids once I was

working as a full-time lawyer and he went pro at playing ball, but ever since he dropped out of school we never talked about it again. I was shocked so once he finished cumming in me he stepped back and pulled his pants up as I sat on my desk trying to understand what just happened.

"Fix your face and get up so you can get back to work. Make sure you get all the hours you can before you quit." He spoke, making me snap out of my trance.

"Quit? Quit for what?" I got down off of the desk and looked at him puzzled.

"You can't work when you are pregnant Mya."

"I can work."

"Not with my kids in you." He chuckled looking at me seriously.

"I didn't ask you to do that. I thought we had an agreement. What happened to that?"

"You sneaky so I need to make sure you can't go nowhere, I love you and I'll be damned if I let anybody else come in and take away what's mine."

I knew Damien felt threatened by Pharaoh , but I didn't know it was this bad. I wasn't even sure that he wanted kids by me. He was so determined on making sure nobody else would want me. He had a smart way in doing so.

"Finish up here and I'll see you at home." He smiled as he finished buckling his pants back up.

When he was finished he walked up to me and kissed me on my forehead before turning around and walking out of the room. Once he left I sat down at my desk dumbfounded about what had just happened. Damien knew for sure that the only way he could keep me was if I had his kid. He was wrong, but I couldn't deal with this right now. It would have to wait until later.

Chapter Nine

PHARAOH

I was pissed to say the least. I knew Mya had somebody else in her life, but he wasn't me. He didn't treat her like I would. He couldn't make her toes curl like I could. He wasn't making her smile like I was. Even though she acted like she didn't like me, I knew she did. I just had to get her to see that life with me would be way better. It was just going to take time.

I sat outside her office for almost ten minutes before I got mad and walked out. Hearing her moan out like that made me feel some type of way. I couldn't be that mad because she wasn't mine, so I had to keep my focus on working with her. I didn't need anything we had going on between us to mess up anything with my trial, so I was going to do just that. Everything was going to be strictly business from here on out.

To get my mind off of Mya I called up Mitch and

told him to meet me at the courts. I quickly made my way home to change my clothes before I made my way there.

Pulling up to the courts, I got out of the car and walked over to one. I saw Mitch at the other end shooting around. I put my hands on my mouth and did the bird call making him turn around and do it back.

"What's up my nigga." He smiled as he jogged up to me, giving me the handshake.

"Nothing *mano*, what are the streets talking about?" I asked, taking the ball from his hands and started dribbling it through my legs before taking a jump shot.

"Shit. Them Valley niggas ain't been popping shit. They are still trying to figure out what happened to ole boy and his girl."

"Well watch your back. Them valley niggas are sneaky as fuck."

"You know me man, I'm always peeping shit even when it ain't nothing to peep."

"Speaking of peeping shit, you remember the girl and her friends I was talking to at the party last month?" I questioned passing him the ball.

"Oh yeah she had a friend named Aaliyah, her name was Nya or some shit like that?" He thought for a second before answering.

"Yeah her name is Mya. Anyway, she with that nigga we kicked off the courts last month."

"Didn't you fuck her though?" He questioned, confused.

"I didn't just fuck her man. I beat her walls loose. Made that pussy remember me" I admitted making him laugh.

"This is the same girl working on your case right?"

"Yeah see that's the problem, I don't need whatever me and her got going on to fuck with anything I got going on. You know the prosecutor peep everything."

"So cut whatever you got going on with her out, you don't need anything else distracting you from making shit happen. We already trying to get these Valley niggas out of the way. We almost got the Valley in our pocket. We just need to finish taking care of a couple more people and then we straight. Her nigga a Valley boy ain't he?" Mitch asked, looking at me.

"Yeah, but I'm not even worried about all that. I know for a fact that he is hitting on her and she doesn't deserve that." I spoke checking up on him.

Just being able to play ball and talk about everything that was going on in my life made me feel at peace.

"She doesn't, but you can't make her leave him to be with you because if you could, you would have her by now. You fucked her and all that, but she gotta see that he is not right for her on her own. If she doesn't leave him on her own he will always be there to get her back. You see how easy it was for her to cheat on him with you?"

Mitch was right. I would just have to wait until she made the decision on her own. I just hope he doesn't beat her to death before she has the chance to do it.

"I guess you're right *Mano*, you still coming with me to meet up with Santos at the docks later?"

"For what we just saw him last week! I thought you had him coming through once every month." He looked at me like I was crazy.

"I did until them niggas from the Valley ran up on Nate. Now I got some shit coming in that I know they don't have."

"Oh alright well we don't have to worry about this shit too much longer. Once we find out who and where Tyrone, Caesar, Big Dame are, we will have the West End to the Valley. Can't nobody fuck with us after that."

"You're right." I spoke, nodding my head at his logic.

"I'm always right my nigga."

"Whatever. Come on let's play a quick game to twenty and get up out of here. I don't need Santos at them docks longer than he needs to." I passed him the ball before walking up to him guarding him.

———

"¡*Santos! ¿Qué pasa mi amigo (Santos! What's happening my friend)?*" I asked how he was doing as me and Mitch walked out on the deck to get on the boat.

Santos was a long time associate of mine from Mexico. He worked for me, but he sold his own supply in Mexico. He had every drug you could name and I needed some new shit that niggas in the Valley didn't have access to.

"*Soy genial. ¿Qué necesitas (I am great. What do y'all need)?*" He asked, looking between me and Mitch.

"Man can you two niggas speak English for once? Shit I'm

tired of coming here trying to decode whatever the fuck y'all saying." Mitch interrupted causing me and Santos to buss out laughing.

"Nice to see you, Mitch. How have you been around for this long and still don't know the lingo *Mano?*" Santos questioned once he stopped laughing.

"I know it, but when you niggas get together y'all be talking way to fast." Mitch chuckled and shook his head.

"Lo siento mano (I'm sorry)." Santos spoke really slow, making me laugh.

"Fuck you. What you got for us nigga?" Mitch laughed and waved him off.

"I got any and everything you need. I got weed, cocaína, heroin, meth, xanny's, perc's, oxy, and special k."

"What are you doing? Selling that shit at raves?" I asked once he was finished.

"Everywhere, you would be surprised what people do to get high." He chuckled and shrugged his shoulders.

"What do you think Mitch?" I asked, hoping he had an answer.

"I think we should get the weed, cocaine and meth as usual, and then we should get the Xanny's and perc's. We can get the word out that we got them now and then sell them for ten dollars pill. Them Valley niggas ain't thinking about selling nothing like that."

"Escuchar a su hermano (Listen to your brother)." Santos said nodding his head in agreement telling me to listen to Mitch.

"Alright give me the normal shit and then get me eight hundred of each pill." I gave in and got something new.

"Cool, I'll be right back."

Santos went down to get the supply and then came back up a couple minutes later. After making sure everything was there and handing him his money we were on our way. I had to get this bagged and out on the streets before I headed home for the day. Hopefully my workers knew how to sell all of these damn pills or else this would be a lot of money I had just lost.

When I left the warehouse after making sure everything was getting bagged correctly I headed home. When I pulled into the driveway I could see a car parked right outside my gate. I didn't know who it was because the only person who knew where I lived was Mitch and he was back at the warehouse handling business. I grabbed my gun from my glove compartment and got out of the car. Walking up to the driver side of the car I hid the gun behind my back with one hand and knocked on the window with my free hand. The window started to roll down making me take a step back just in case. When it got halfway down I noticed that it was Mya.

"Damn what's up *bebita?* What are you doing here?" I asked tucking the gun in my pants behind my back.

"You left before we could finish our meeting." She smiled.

She looked good as usual, but I was still pissed about early so I stood there looking at her with a straight face.

"So you bring it to my house?" I questioned.

"Uh yeah, we have to go to court in three days so I need all the time I can get so we can win this."

"Is that right?"

"Yes, can I come in." She asked pouting.

I chuckled and backed up to put the code into the gate before looking back at her telling her to go ahead. I got back in my car and followed behind her all the way in my driveway.

Chapter Ten

MYA

"Your honor the people would like to charge the defendant with illegal drug possession with the intent to distribute, drug trafficking, and manufacturing." The prosecutor stated standing up out of her seat.

"How does the defense plead?" The judge asked once everybody was seated in the courtroom.

"Not guilty, your honor, the defense would like to move to get all charges dropped." I sternly spoke standing up out of my seat.

Today was the day that made or broke my career as a defense attorney. I understood that you win some and lose some, but this was my first case and I wanted to win.

"Objection, your honor the defendant was caught with multiple pounds of marijuana in his possession." The prosecutor spoke briefly looking at me like I was insane.

"Your honor when my client was pulled over in a routine traffic stop he had two joints for medicinal purposes in which he had a medical license. The rest was in a sealed bag in which the LAPD had no right to check. There was no warrant presented when Officer Willis checked my defendants car. So these so-called pounds of marijuana shouldn't even be admissible in court." I spoke with high confidence as I looked the judge directly in the eye.

The judge sat there for a couple of seconds trying to collect his thoughts before sighing deeply.

"Since there was no warrant present to the defendant when Officer Willis searched the vehicle I have no choice but to withdraw the concealed bag as evidence and drop the charges. You got lucky this time Mr. Rivera don't let me catch you in here again. Court is adjourned, you are free to go." The Judge banged his gavel and stood to leave.

I looked over at Jessica and Pharaoh and smiled. I had just won my first case and it felt amazing. I had no idea that it would be this fast but a win is a win.

"Nice going kid, you just left the best prosecutor's mouth hanging open." Jessica walked up to me and smiled, shaking my hand.

"Thank you." I smiled ear to ear.

"So, now that this is over would you come out and celebrate with me? It's just a small lunch." Pharaoh asked standing up from his seat.

I was so busy trying to focus on winning this case, I hadn't paid attention to how good he looked in his court clothes. He had on a black button up and black slacks with holes in the knees, a red blazer and a matching red belt.

"I have some paperwork to finish." I spoke thinking of an excuse.

"No you don't, I'll finish it, you go out and enjoy your win." Jessica butted in as she packed up all of the paperwork into her briefcase and left the courtroom.

"Let me thank you *bebita*." Pharaoh stuck his hand out for me.

I stood there for a second before giving in and grabbing his hand in mine.

"Just this one time, and don't try anything." I pointed my finger at him as I picked up my purse to go.

"I won't try anything you don't want me to." He chuckled before turning around and walking out of the courtroom.

I followed him out of the courtroom shaking my head. I knew that statement was as sarcastic as they could get but I ignored it.

———

*W*alking into the restaurant, I looked around at how dark and beautiful it looked on the inside. The only lights that were on were the ones above the tables. It was still lit enough to see what was going on in front of you.

Pharaoh held onto me by the nape of my back as we

walked up to the host booth. When the host saw us coming he smiled and grabbed the menu before welcoming us.

"Welcome back Mr. Rivera, would you like your normal booth this evening?" He questioned looking between Pharaoh and I.

"Yeah, and can I also get your oldest bottle of *Dominio de Pingus* (Expensive wine from spain.) when you get a chance?" Pharaoh answered.

"Yes, right this way." The host responded.

Walking up to the table on the balcony outside, I smiled at the view. It was high, so I could see the Hollywood sign in the distance. Pharaoh pulled my chair out for me and I sat down in amazement because that was another thing Damien didn't do. Once he sat down Pharaoh just looked at me through hooded eyes. He didn't say anything, he just continued to stare.

"Why are you looking at me like that?" I questioned finally breaking the silence.

"You look beautiful today, you always look beautiful. It's just something about you today that I don't know about." He shook his head and leaned back in his seat still looking at me.

"What does that even mean?" I questioned with a chuckle.

"I'm guessing that your dude has been treating you right."

Pharaoh had guessed right Damien has been sweet to me the past couple of weeks but the whole knocking me up just so I would stay, had me feeling some type of way. Yes I wanted kids, but now wasn't the right time. I still had to figure myself out, so I decided to take the morning after pill right after I left my office that day.

"He has." I smiled at the thought.

"That's good, I'm glad he's making you happy again." He tried to hide the look of disappointment but it didn't work.

I was going to comment on it but I decided to drop it. I looked at him for a second before picking up the menu and looking at it.

"What are you going to eat?" I asked peeking up from my menu.

"I like how you did that, but I'm probably going to get the fish tacos. What are you thinking about getting?" Pharaoh questioned.

"Oh I don't know. Damien normally picks my food for me."

"Well he is not here right now so pick whatever you like."

"Oh okay then I'll have the shrimp Alfredo." I smiled down at the menu.

———

*A*fter getting our food, we decided to sit and talk since every time we did have time to talk with just the two of us, it never lasted for very long.

"So what made you want to become a defense attorney?" Pharaoh dropped his fork on his plate and looked up at me.

"I used to watch so much tv when I was younger. The first

48 and Law and Order. I realized that sometimes the system does send innocent people to jail sometimes because they always give them one of those public defenders. I wanted to be a defense attorney to keep innocent people with not a lot of money out of jail."

"You do know that most of the time the people who you will be defending will be guilty of what they are accused of?" He questioned again.

"Yes that's why I read over their files before I make my decision to be their lawyer." I drank some of my wine as I answered his question

"So you got everything figured out?"

"Yes, well at least almost. What do you do for a living?"

"I'm what they call an entrepreneur of sorts. I sell a lot of services and make a profit in return." He smirked at his own response.

"What services do you sell?"

"Medicinal services, everything I sell temporarily makes the pain go away."

"So like a pharmacist?" I questioned, still confused making him laugh.

"Yeah a pharmacist, I guess you can say that." He spoke, nodding his head and picking up his wine.

"Do you have a girlfriend?" I questioned making him stop drinking and look at me.

"If I'm trying my best to make you mine, why would I be stringing some girl around while I do it?"

"Because I'm in a relationship so I don't want you to wait on me."

"Like I said before, there's something about you that I don't know about. You haven't been treated like you supposed to and I'm here to make you understand that. It might take a minute but you something special and I'm willing to wait for you to see that you deserve way better than what you've been getting." He spoke sincerely.

I wasn't expecting that response so I sat there looking at Pharaoh until I made sense of the whole thing. I never had anybody, but Damien show me this kind of attention so I really didn't know how to handle it. I was glad when his phone started to ring because it stopped the awkward silence.

"¿Qué pasa?" Pharaoh answered his phone in Spanish.

I couldn't make out what the person on the other end of the phone was saying, but I could tell that it was making him mad.

"No vayas a ninguna parte, estaré allí en treinta minutos (Don't go anywhere, I'll be there in thirty minutes)."

Listening to him talk in Spanish was sexy even though all I understood was don't go anywhere. When he hung up the phone he reached into his pocket and pulled out a wad of cash. He took a couple bills off the top and sat them down on top of the table before standing up.

"I have to get up out of here, are you ready?" He asked, sticking his hand out for mine.

"Yeah let's go." I stood up and we walked outside.

Pulling up on the curb next to my house, Pharaoh killed the engine and looked over at me.

"Call me if you need me, I'll talk to you later." He caressed my cheek and then kissed my forehead before pulling back and smiling at me.

I got out of the car and waved goodbye before walking into the house.

Chapter Eleven

PHARAOH

"Why is it that everytime I come to collect from you, it's always a problem?" I questioned Mark, the club owner as I held my 9mm to his temple.

Since Mitch was my right hand man he did all of my dirty work. That meant collecting my cut from all of the bars and strip clubs in town. To get more people coming in and more money in their club they call me to sell and promote. Every week Mitch comes to collect my profit and from time to time he had to let people know that I wasn't the one to play with. Either you had all of my money on time or you didn't. If you didn't then you had to answer to my 9.

"I swear I just counted it and it was all there." He rushed out with his hands in the air.

"I just counted it too and it's not all there. You got 2 seconds to give me the rest of my money or else somebody will be cleaning you up off the walls." I pressed the gun to his temple making him jump.

Usually Mitch would wait until he left to count the money, but since Mark's money has been short for three weeks I told him to count it in front of him.

Mark continued to look at me like he didn't understand what I was saying, so I cocked my gun and aimed it between his eyes.

"You really want to try me today Mark?" I questioned through gritted teeth.

"No, No please. Here this is the rest of it." He quickly reached into his pocket and pulled out a rolled stack of money that was tied with a rubber band.

I chuckled and snatched the roll out of his hand before punching him in the face with my free hand.

"Mark, Mark, Mark." I watched as he fell out of his seat and onto the floor. "I never met a *vato* that was so ready to die in my life." I shook my head as he tried to get up off of the floor.

"I'm sorry, it won't happen again." He whined from the floor.

"Yeah I know it won't."

Just as he got off of the floor I raised my 9 and pulled the trigger. I unloaded my clip into his chest before sending the last bullet to his head. I was done playing games with him.

Walking out of Mark's office, I put the gun in my waistband and walked out of the bar with Mitch trailing behind me. It was only 2 o'clock in the afternoon so his bar wasn't even open yet. Nobody knew about what Mitch and I did around town except for the people who worked with us, so nobody would find out what happened Mark.

The Los Angeles sun burned bright as I made my way to my car to call cleanup. I had to let them know about Mark.

"What up Ro, how was court?" He asked as the phone connected.

"What up Q, it was straight I just finished handling business. Get Ty and y'all come down to Mark's. I need it cleaned and ready when it opens tonight." I answered as I stood by my car and started it up.

"You got it boss." With that he hung up the phone.

I turned around and looked at Mitch who was smiling and texting on his phone.

"The fuck is you over there smiling and shit for?" I questioned popping the locks on my car.

"None of yo business Nigga. You coming out with the crew tonight?"

"Man you know I don't really get down like that no more."

"What if I told you that Ceaser and that nigga Dame supposed to be there?" He smirked knowing that I would say yes then.

"Alright man I'll go. They better be there too."

"Bet meet me at my house and you can follow me and Trey there."

"Why the fuck is Trey coming? You know that he doesn't know how to act."

Trey was Mitch's little brother. He was nineteen and didn't

listen to anything anybody had to say. Plus he was trigger happy so if you looked at him wrong or said the wrong thing he was ready to shoot.

"Cause he won a bet and I told him we might need the extra help tonight.

"Man alright. You watching that lil o-dog looking nigga too."

"Alright man, meet me at my house at eleven."

"Alright." With that I got in my car and drove off.

Tonight was going to be interesting.

———

"*Can I touch that booty? That booty, that big ol' booty*"
The club shook as *Booty by Blac Youngsta blared through the speakers.* Instead of chilling in VIP or dancing on the floor with everybody else, I sat at the bar with my back turned towards the crowd. I watched all the people dancing while I sipped on my third glass of circo as I looked around at the girls dancing and moving their bodies effortlessly.

At one point in time I was in love with shit like this. Women in general had me mesmerized with them. Anything they said or did had me wrapped around their pinky fingers. I'd fuck any girl that was willing and able, and then never really thought about or remembered it the next day. I made it out of the hood and a lot of people knew it. Women only wanted what came from being with me. I'd buy a girl every-thing she asked for, all she had to do was ask. It started to feel like they were only there for me to buy them stuff. It started to get old and I didn't want to spend my money on people who weren't giving me the satisfaction I needed in return. The pussy was good but as I got older I knew I needed more than that.

Only thing that changed was, I wasn't in the hood any more. Me and my niggas made it out while others stayed and if they did they weren't making as much money as I was making. I was the little skinny light skin *niño* from the grove. I lost my virginity by the age of thirteen, and by the age of fifteen I was selling cocaine and weed in California and Mexico. Bought my mom and dad a house at the age of eighteen because I knew it was the only reason they would let me stop going to school. From day one school wasn't for me. I'm far from dumb, I know a lot of shit but I didn't have go to school and learn it. Everything I needed to know was right here in the streets and I was doing good.

"So you come to the club just to sit and watch everybody have fun?" Came from the side of me, knocking me out of my thoughts.

Mya was standing with her back towards the crowd looking at me. I took another sip of my drink and focused my attention back on the crowd.

"I'm not really here to have fun. Who are you here with?" I questioned looking over at her briefly.

"My girls. They wanted to take me out to enjoy my first win. You want to come hang with us?" She asked, tilting her head to the side.

"Where y'all at?"

"Down stairs VIP come on." She held her hand out and I thought for a second before grabbing her hand and standing up.

We made our way through the crowd as I followed behind Mya as she held my hand. I couldn't help but look at her ass as it jiggled a little in the tight leather leggings she had on. It reminded me of when I had her in my bed and my hands touched every inch of her.

I shook the thoughts of Mya out of my head before we walked into the downstairs VIP.

"Hey girls, look who I found." Mya called out, making everybody who was in VIP stop and look at us.

"Oop, look Aaliyah she went to go get some drinks and came back with a snack." Mya's friend Kris said, giving her the side eye.

"Pharaoh you remember Kris and Aaliyah?" She asked, trying to sit down but I pulled her back to me.

I sat down first before pulling her onto my lap comfortably.

"Yeah I do. How are you ladies doing tonight?" I asked, resting my hand on her legs.

"We are good, but I was wondering if you happened to bring your friend from last time here with you?" Aaliyah asked hopefully.

"Yeah he upstairs, handling some business for me, you can probably go up there and chill with him. Just tell the guard Ro sent you up."

"Y'all got bottles up there?" Her other friend Kris asked.

"Yeah we got bottles." I chuckled at how excited he looked.

"Come on hoe, we're going to kick it with some ballers," Kris quickly stood up and yanked Aaliyah up with him. "We will be upstairs if you need us YaYa."

They left, leaving only me and Mya as the only ones in the room.

"So you telling me that you got a whole VIP area with bottles and you decided to stay at the bar by yourself drinking by yourself?" Mya asked me after a moment of silence.

"Yeah, I told you I'm here to handle business plus I'm not with the whole club scene anymore. I don't like a lot of people."

"I see that, but you decided to come in here with me." She spoke turning a little on my lap as she looked at me.

"Yeah, that's because you pulled me in here against my will plus you weren't going to leave me alone if I didn't." I chuckled.

Chapter Twelve

MYA

"Don't act like you don't like being with me." I chuckled as I relaxed my nerves while I sat on Pharaoh's lap.

"I really don't but you look good as fuck right now so I'm straight." He licked his lips and smiled at me.

I knew now he was lying about enjoying my company, but was hard to tell because he kept a straight face most of the time.

"Thank you, don't look half bad yourself." I chuckled nervously

"Yeah alright. Where yo boy?"

"Who Damien?"

"If that's what you call him." He shrugged his shoulder and looked up at me.

"He went to go handle business."

"That's what they call it nowadays?" He asked squinting at me.

"What is that supposed to mean?"

"Nothing so how come-" Pharaoh was cut off by his phone ringing.

He quickly slid it out of his pocket to answer it. I was about to get up to let him take his call, but he wrapped his arms around my waist and pulled me closer.

"You saw both of them? Where at? Alright tell them to let them in and don't do nothing until I get up there. Bet I'll be out in a second." He hung up the phone and sat it on the side of him before wrapping his arms around me.

"Come on let's find your girls and you can hit my line when you make it home tonight. I gotta go handle some business outside." He turned my head towards him and then pecked my lips twice. His lips were so soft that I wanted more, but my mind wandered off to Damien so instead of kissing him again I got up off of Pharaoh's lap. He stood up and smiled at me briefly before extending his hand out for mine. I grabbed a hold on his hand and we walked out of the room together.

I had the biggest smile on my face as me and Pharaoh walked out of the downstairs VIP room. The VIP room was in a whole separate area of the club, so it only had couches and chairs and tables and its own separate stereo system. All of the windows were tinted so the people inside the VIP could see out into the crowd but the crowd couldn't see in. That's how I spotted Pharaoh sitting at the bar. I sat watching him for thirty minutes before I went out to talk to him. It looked like he was in his own little world not worrying about anything around him. Kris and Aaliyah spotted him too, and once I had told them about what really happened the last time we went out and I disappeared, they talked me into going to talk to him. They don't know Pharaoh at all and they swore he was a good person. I guess at this point they would rather I talk to anybody but Damien. I had finally told them that he had been hitting on me. Of course they already knew, but they both said that I can't be heard if I didn't speak up. They said that if I couldn't come out and say it, they didn't know if I needed their help.

As Pharaoh and I weaved through the crowd my phone started ringing. I looked to see Damien calling, I instantly ignored it. For all he knew I was at home sleeping, and I didn't need him finding out where I was and who I was with. A couple seconds after that Kris was calling me I ignored it thinking he was just being nosy.

We walked up the stairs to the VIP room where two guards stood manning the door.

"*¿Qué pasa, los dejaste entrar* (What 's up? You let them in)?" Pharaoh spoke in his native slang.

"Si, señor." They answered back.

"*Bein, no dejes que nadie más entre* (Good don't let anyone else in)," He said before the guards moved out of the way to let us through.

When we opened the door to walk in, a huge cloud of smoke exited. Pharaoh held onto my hand as we walked over to the couches where everybody was. The only lights that were in the room were strobe lights that bounced off the walls. We walked up and Pharaoh dapped Mitch up.

"Where are they at?" He questioned as he sat down and pulled me on his lap.

"Over there at the bar drinking and shit, what are you thinking about doing?" Mitch asked, sparking the blunt he was holding in his hands.

Before Pharaoh could say anything else, I was yanked off his lap. I looked up to see who Kris and Aaliyah both were looking at me with worried looks on their face.

"What is wrong with y'all why are y'all looking at me like that?" I questioned pulling my arm away from Kris.

"Well if you would answer your phone sometimes, you would know that Damien is here in this room. You lucky Aaliyah vampire ass saw you in the dark before Damien did."

"Yeah had me squinting at everything that walked into this room. Making my head hurt." Aaliyah added to rubbing her temple.

My heart started beating and I barely understood what they said to me after I heard that Damien was here. I stood there looking around trying to see if I could find him and when I looked over at the bar he was sitting there looking dead at me. I knew he was looking at me because he got up and started walking over to me. I continued to look at him as he made his way over to me. He looked down at his phone and then put it up to his ear, and a couple seconds later my phone started ringing.

"He is coming over her-." I tried to tell Kris and Aaliyah, but was cut off by Pharaoh wrapping his arms around my waist and pulling me close, as he pecked my lips a couple times.

"What's wrong bebita?" He noticed that I was stiff and tense.

Instead of answering him I looked back at Damien who was fuming. I had never seen him this mad before in my life. Kris and Aaliyah noticed me looking off into the distance and turned around to see who I was looking at. When they saw Damien coming they tried to hide me, but it was too late I was already caught.

"Oh shit let me make sure my wig is okay cause shit is about to hit the fan." Kris said fixing his wig just as Damien walked up to us.

"Oh so this what the fuck we doing now Mya?" Damien asked as he grabbed my wrist and yanked me away from Pharaoh and started walking out of the club.

"Ouch! Damien you're hurting me." I shouted over the music and tried to yank my arm away from him to no avail.

Once we made it outside of the club, I finally freed myself from his grasp and stopped walking. Damein stopped but instead of grabbing me again, he turned around and punched me right in the nose sending me falling to the floor holding onto my bleeding nose.

"I told your dumb ass to stay in the fucking house and then I come to the club and catch you smiling in another nigga face," He kicked me hard in my stomach knocking what little breath I had left in me.

"Not only did you ignore my calls, you were hugged up with the same nigga I keep telling you to stay away from." He hit me a couple of times, hard across my body.

"You really think I'm fucking stupid, I'll kill both of y'all. You lucky we in public because I'd kill your stupid ass right now." He sneered as he hit me a couple more times.

I tried to hold onto my nose to stop it from bleeding and block his punches that were coming one after the other but it wasn't working. Just then I heard somebody running towards us. I looked up just in enough time to see Damien being tackled to the ground by Pharaoh. It was Damien's turn to get beat on as Pharaoh angrily stood over him sending blow after blow. I sat there trying to catch my breath as Pharaoh beat Damien's head into the ground.

As much as Damien deserved it, I couldn't let Pharaoh continue to hit him so I got up off of the ground to stop it.

"Pharaoh stop, he's going to go unconscious please." I grabbed a hold of Pharaoh making him stop and look back at me.

"You okay?" Pharaoh questioned walking up to me to see if I was okay.

He cupped my face and looked me over.

"Yes I'm fine, but he's not." I moved Pharaoh's hands from my face as Damien began to regain his composure.

I rushed over to Damien and held his head to my chest.

"Baby you okay?" I asked, trying to wipe the blood from his lip.

"He good, come on *bebita* let's get you cleaned up," Pharaoh grabbed my shoulder, but I shrugged him off as I tried to help Damien up off of the ground.

"I have to make sure he's okay." I snapped back at Pharaoh.

"I'm just trying to help you out." He spoke sounding hurt.

"I never asked you for your help. So please leave me alone and let me get him home please," I spat standing up with Damien's arm slung over my shoulder.

"I'll leave you alone, you don't have to worry about me but when he beats yo ass to where you damn near dead. Don't fucking call me cause remember you don't need my help." He looked at me in disgust before turning around and walking back into the club.

I watched the club doors close before smiling up at Damien as he tried to stand up on his own.

"Come on baby let's get you home."

Chapter Thirteen

PHARAOH

"Where the fuck did you just go? Where that nigga Dame just go?" Mitch asked as I walked back into the VIP room.

I was beyond pissed about what just happened outside of the club that I had forgotten my whole point in even coming here.

"You mean to tell me Dame and Damien are the same fucking people?" I semi yelled in the room as I looked at Mitch.

He nodded his head. I dropped my head and sighed. I had this nigga right in my grasp and now this nigga gone. I knew where he lived so it was just a matter of time before I caught him again. For right now I had other shit to handle. I was going to take these Valley nigga's down one by one so they knew what the fuck was going on.

"Mya is his girl and she took him home after I beat the fuck out of him in the parking lot, where that nigga Caesar at? He's still in here?" I asked Mitch looking around the room.

"Yeah he's over there at the bar."

"Alright, I don't care what you have to do, but grab that nigga and take him back to the spot. I need everything they took from Nate when they killed him you got that?" I asked to make sure he understood what I was saying.

"Yeah, you know I got you my nigga."

"Alright call me when you got him, I'm about to head out I got some other shit I need to do." I spoke looking around the room.

I was looking for Mya's friends when I saw them sitting at the chairs in the corner looking worried. I walked over to them so I could let them know what had just happened. I wasn't sure if they knew what had been going on between Mya and Damien, but they needed to know so they could probably be able to help her.

"Can y'all come with me real quick?" I asked and they both looked up at me like I was crazy. "I think Mya is in trouble, Damien was just beating her out in the parking lot when I went to check on her and I jumped in to help her. She told me to stop and that she didn't need my help. Maybe y'all can help before she gets herself killed."

When I said that they both popped up off of the couch and started walking toward the exit.

"Do you know if they went home?" Kris asked, stopping and turning around to ask me.

"Yeah I think so." I answered nodding my head.

"Good because I got a key. Damien in for a bogo."

"Kris what are you going to do and what the fuck is a bogo?" Aaliyah asked, looking at him confused.

"Bitch he is going to get this left hook and get this right one for free the fuck." He spoke before opening the door and walking out of the VIP room.

Aaliyah laughed and I just shook my head as I made my way down the stairs and out of the club. I didn't have a problem with niggas like Kris, because whoever they wanted to be in life had nothing to do with me. If he liked dudes it was up to him, that is what made him happy. What he identified himself as made no difference in my life, as long as he knew where he stood with me.

When we made it outside, I told them that they could ride with me and I would bring them back to their car. The car was silent as we rode down the street to Mya's house. Halfway there, three police cars zoomed past us and soon after an ambulance came zooming past as well. I tried to see where they were going, but I had to slow down because traffic was backed up. Once we got closer to what was going on Aaliyah screamed and pointed out of the passenger side window. I looked over to see a car that had driven off of the road and into the side of a brick building.

"That's Mya's car." She held her hands up to her mouth and started to cry.

"Are you sure?" I questioned looking over at her briefly.

"Yes I'm sure. She has had that car for years." She answered histerically.

When she said that I quickly backed up a little and drove around to get closer to the scene. Once I was closer, I turned the car off and looked over at Aaliyah as tears fell from her eyes.

"Stop crying I'm about to go see what's up, y'all two stay in the car until I get back alright." I looked between the two of them before they nodded their heads.

I got out of the car and walked closer to where the EMT's were taking the gurney's out of the car. I continued to walk closer until a policeman stopped me by putting his hand on my chest.

"You have to take a step back sir."

"I think that's my friend Mya, I just saw her at the club and told her to go home. Is that her?" I questioned trying to look over his shoulder.

"Well sir I can't let you through but you can follow the EMT's to the hospital." Just as he said that, the EMT's started pulling bodies from the car.

I took a step back and just watched worried if it was really her. When they pulled the body out of the passenger seat I could tell right off the back that it was Mya. I could tell by the clothes she had on, and I couldn't believe it. When they put her on the gurney she started moving around I felt a little better. Since she looked like she was okay, I walked back to my car so I could let her friends know and follow the EMT's.

When I got back in the car it was quiet and they were waiting for me to talk.

"It looks like she is okay, I'm going to drop y'all off at the hospital and I gotta go handle some shit, y'all cool with that?" I looked between the two of them.

"Yeah, it's fine, as long as Mya is okay." Aaliyah answered.

"What she said," Kris added.

I nodded my head and started the car and waited for the EMT's to finish what they were doing and pull off so that I could follow behind them.

———

"Where is my money Ceasar?" I questioned as I paced back and forth in front of him.

I knew what I got from the last nigga I killed wasn't everything that they took from Nate when they killed him. I needed everything that was mine back even if that meant a lot of people would have to die before I could get it.

"Jay had it, all of it. I keep telling you that." He answered slowly as he tried to catch his breath.

"You don't think I know that you and Jay ran up on my nigga and then split that shit between y'all and the niggas that set it all up? You know what ay Mitch?"

"What's up G?" Mitch asked as he sat on the table across the room smoking a blunt.

"Pass me that machete." I smiled as Mitch's eyes lit up.

"You need me to put the plastic down?" He quickly hopped off the table.

"Yeah it's going to get a little messy." I laughed as he quickly handed me the knife and then started putting plastic on the floor.

"Come on man y'all ain't gotta do all this I told y'all everything y'all wanted to know." Caesar looked back and forth between me and Mitch frantically.

"See and that's the problem. You told us everything but the truth, and now I gotta show you that I don't like being lied to." I raised the Machete in the air before bringing it down hard onto Caesar's hand making him scream out in pain as his hand fell to the floor beside him.

"Damn nigga, yo thirsty ass couldn't have waited until I was finished putting the plastic down?" Mitch asked over Caesar's screams.

"Nah, I couldn't. Ay C so are you going to lie to me again and lose another limb or are you going to tell me the truth?" I asked, twisting the machete in my hands.

"The rest of the money is in my safe house in the valley. 2678 faresdrive rd my cut is there. I don't know where the rest of it is."

"See now was that so hard?" I questioned as I stopped and stood in front of him.

Before he could answer I stopped twirling the knife in my hand and swung it like a baseball bat at his head sending it flying across the room. I was done playing the games with everybody. It was time for me to reclaim what was mine.

"Get Q and Ty over here to clean him up. I'm about to head back out to the hospital."

I had told him all about the Mya situation while he was beating Ceaser up and tying him to the chair.

"Alright G, let me know what happens." Mitch answered as I started to walk out of the room.

"*No problema Mano*" I waved him off as I kicked Cesar's head back to where his body was on the way out.

Chapter Fourteen

MYA- EIGHT HOURS EARLIER...

"I'm alright, I can drive," Damien let go of me and walked over to the driver side door.

I watched as he winced in pain as he tried to close the door. I felt bad about what happened to Damien because it was all my fault. I didn't mean for him to catch me out, especially since Pharaoh was there.

Once I got in the car and buckled myself in Damien sped out of the parking lot and down the street. I started to get scared when the car continued to speed down the street.

"Damien you're going too fast, slow down." I spoke looking over at him nervously.

He gripped the steering wheel and his jaw clenched, but he showed no emotion.

"You don't love me no more Mya huh? Is that what it is?" He asked, taking his eyes off of the road briefly.

"What are you talking about Damien? I do love you." I answered looking between him and the road.

"You do really? I mean cause if you did you wouldn't have gotten rid of my baby and then you see what the fuck that nigga did to me over you huh? A nigga that you swear you not fucking with, but everywhere he show up you not that far behind him. You must think I fucking stupid huh?"

Damien was talking calmly but I could tell by the way his jaw clenched and tears fell from his eyes that he was far from calm. I had no idea that he had found out I had gotten rid of the baby, and now that he knew I couldn't say anything that would change it.

"No Damien you're not stupid. You and I both know that we can't have a kid right now, we are not ready for one right now." I spoke softly trying to get him to slow down.

"You are not ready! I told you I was ready for this Mya. I want to be with you for the rest of my life and you don't understand that. You are not leaving me and I can't let nobody else have you."

He looked over at me just as he pressed the gas harder, running off of the road.

"Damien!" I screamed and brassed myself as we ran right into a brick wall.

———

"*Y*ou weren't going to do nothing Kris stop lying." Aaliyah laughed.

"Don't forget I'm a nigga first sweetheart would have popped these nails off and beat his motherfucking ass honey don't play hoe. Only reason why I didn't do anything before is because Mya slow ass lying and shit trying to protect him. Even though he wasn't giving a fuck about her when he was beating her ass up." Kris sucked his teeth.

I could hear the two talking about me before I had even opened my eyes and tried to look around but couldn't.

"Yeah that was just dumb because all she had to do was speak up and I would have called my cousins Mookie and PJ. You remember when Mookie and Damien fought because Mookie liked her to." Aaliyah went on not paying attention to me.

"Damien got his ass beat then and I'm pretty sure he didn't want to relive that L." Kris said, making me snicker and the hiss in pain.

They both looked over at me and saw that I was awake before they rushed over to my side. They looked at me like they were scared to touch me and I started to tear up.

"How bad is it?" I asked, my voice raspy and my mouth was dry.

"You want honesty? If so you look fucking awful bitch. You need to get it together." Kris blurted out making Aaliyah reach across the, and hit him in his shoulder.

"You are such an asshole." She said, shaking her head.

"What I'm just stating facts, but at least she looks better than when he was beating her ass."

"You just can't stop can you Kris?" Aaliyah asked, sounding like a mom.

"No I cannot, but how are you feeling Tina?" Kris questioned looking at me dead serious.

"I'm sore, can you get me some water, and my name is not Tina hoe." I shot back.

"Could have fooled me. Anyway you should be sore, your ribs are bruised and you have a broken leg." Kris blurted out.

"Kris!" Aaliyah yelled causing him to give her the stank face.

"What hoe why do you insist on calling my name so much damn. How about you make yourself useful and go get the damn nurse." Kris sucked his teeth and rolled his eyes.

"Could y'all two stop! Here I am near death in a hospital and y'all want to go back and forth with each other. Aaliyah go get the nurse and Kris go make yourself useful and get me some water." I yelled at them before screaming out in pain because of how bad my body hurt.

"Eww both you don't have to be so rude, that's why you laid up in the hospital now with your broken ass." Kris interjected, scrunching his face up at me.

"What's all this yelling about in here?" The nurse walked in with Pharaoh close behind him.

When they saw that I was awake they rushed over to the bed. Pharaoh looked slightly worried but not too much.

"How are you feeling?" The nurse asked, raising my bed up so that I could look like I was sitting up.

"Sore, and these two aren't making it any better." I answered rolling my eyes at both Aaliyah and Kris.

"Well I got some news for you, do you want me to wait

until it's just me and you." The nurse questioned as he checked my vitals.

"We are all family. Anything I find out they will know about it eventually."

"Okay well as you may know already. You have a couple of minor injuries which include a bruised rib sand your right leg is broken. I'm glad you had your seatbelt on because that's saved your baby from impact." He started, making me look up at him like he was crazy.

I was confused and thankful at the same time. I had no idea that I was even pregnant since I took plan B with Damien. The only other person I had sex with was Pharaoh.

"Do you happen to know how far along I am?" I questioned looking directly at Pharaoh who just continued to look at me.

If I was more than a month then the baby was Pharaoh's anything other than that the plan B didn't work and I was carrying the child of a man who abused me for years.

The nurse looked over his clipboard unsure before he pointed and squinted at the piece of paper.

"I see here that you are about nine weeks along." He looked up at me as he answered.

I looked at Pharaoh who had a look on his face as if to say he understood what that meant.

"Oh my god I'm going to be an auntie!" Kris screamed out, causing everyone in the room to look at him.

"Kris let's go, you need to calm down." Aaliyah shook her head and tried to grab Kris's hand but he pulled it away

"Bitch I will go on my own accord." He stank faced her and then looked at me.

"Kris go." I spoke sternly.

"Fine I'll leave this time but next time I won't." He rolled his eyes and walked out of the room as Aaliyah walked out behind him.

"Hey can you give us a minute?" I asked the nurse once they left.

"Yeah sure. I'll be back to check up on you in thirty minutes." He smiled at me and Pharaoh before he turned and walked out of the room.

Once the door closed behind him I looked at Pharaoh who was typing away on his phone. A couple minutes went by and he had yet to look up from his phone or say anything.

"So are you going to say something?" I asked, making him look up from his phone.

I knew he was mad at me and I knew I was the last person he wanted to talk to right now, but the fact that he was standing in my hospital room meant a lot. It meant he cared cause if he didn't he wouldn't be here.

"My fault. So what happened?" He questioned putting his phone in his pocket.

"He said he could drive home so not thinking anything of it I let him drive. When we got farther from the club he started talking about how he couldn't live without me and couldn't nobody have me. Before I could say anything he ran into the side of the building and now I'm here." I explained.

"Have they told you that he came out of that car with a

couple scars and bruises but no broken bones?" He questioned.

"No."

"Well he ain't make it out of that car alive."

"He died?" I asked not understanding what he was saying.

"Yeah you don't have to worry about him anymore. He is not going to hurt you ever again. You can stay with me if you want." He looked at me sincerely.

"I'm going to have to if you and I are going to get better for our baby."

"So you know for sure that it's mine?" He asked with uncertainty.

"Yes because I took plan B the day me and Damjen did it in my office and I know that since I'm two months along I know for sure it's yours."

"Well then I'm here for you a hundred percent and-"

Before he could finish his sentence the door to my room opened and his friend Mitch stuck his head through.

"My bad for interrupting, but Ro I found where he at, and if you want to handle that we need to do this shit right now." He spoke in code as he looked at Pharaoh.

"Alright I'll be out there in a second." Pharaoh looked back at him.

"Bet, hey Mya you look good." Mitch joked before closing the door.

"I'm going to be back up here a little later. I'm going to see if I can take you home with me tonight. You cool with that?" Pharaoh asked as he slowly walked backwards to the door.

"Yeah I'm cool with that." I smiled as he opened the door and left.

I laid back in my bed and closed my eyes. I was going to take a nap because being in a car accident made me tired and sore.

Chapter Fifteen
PHARAOH

"Well well well if it isn't Big Dame, that's what they call you right *Vato?*" I smiled at Damien as he looked between me and Mitch like he didn't know what was going on.

When I had found that this nigga was still alive after everything that Mya had told me, and what he did to Nate. I had to make sure today was his last day on earth.

"Where am I and why do y'all corny niggas got me naked and tied to a pole? Y'all on some gay shit." He spat us making me and Mitch look at each other and start laughing.

"You owe me a hundred my nigga I told you he was going to say that shit." Mitch laughed and held his hand out for his money.

I had bet that he would ask where Mya was first and

Mitch bet that he would ask why he was naked and tied to a pole.

"You are asking the wrong questions right now. You should be worried about Mya and if she is okay." I answered handing Mitch his money and then focusing my attention back on Damien.

"You better not fucking hurt her." He tried to jump at me but since his hands were bound above his head and his feet were tied together and dangling off the ground he looked like a fish out of water.

"See that's the difference between me and you. I would never lay my hands on that pretty little body of hers. See me I tried to build her up and you continued to beat her down. You ain't gotta worry about her no more though. I'm going to take good care of her and my baby that you almost killed. That's not even why you're here though. What I want to know is where is your cut of the money you stole from me?" I questioned seriously.

"I ain't steal no money from you man let me go." He shook again and Mitch laughed.

"Stop shaking them fucking chains man you not going nowhere." Mitch spat.

"So you don't remember setting up my nigga Nate up." I asked.

"Yeah I remember that, but I ain't know he was with y'all."

"Nigga how you ain't know when he was there with us when you shot up our fucking courts." Mitch butted in looking at Damien like he was stupid.

"Okay okay I had him setup, but I backed out at the last minute so Tyrone ain't split it with me. Jay and Cesar were supposed to go in to grab everything. Nobody was supposed to die." He confessed looking up at me.

"How was nobody supposed to die when they shot my nigga up over forty times?" I inquired.

"It wasn't set up for people to get killed." He confessed.

"Somehow I don't believe you man. I don't even believe you the mastermind behind all of this either. You a pussy nigga and if it got a dick between their legs you ain't popping shit. You weak as fuck and I want you to feel and understand everything that's about to happen to you." I whistled and Chloe and Chaos came running into the room.

They ran up to Mitch and wagged their tails and jumped on him to say hey and then they ran over to me and stood on each side of me. I looked down at them and rubbed their heads before looking up at Damien.

"You know dogs are the best weapon when you train them the right way. They would never turn on you or your family, but all I have to say is one word and they will attack the person they are not familiar with. Everybody is a threat to me so they are ready at all times. To answer your question you asked earlier, you naked because clothing is hard for them to swallow." I smiled devilishly at the way Damien's eyes popped open and began to water.

"Wait wait wai-." He begged, but I really didn't feel like hearing him talk anymore.

"¡COMAN! (EAT!)" I yelled and Chloe and Chaos sprang into attack mode.

They ran up to Damien who was screaming for his life, and jumped on him latching their jaws on him. He screamed out in pain as they continued to bite him.

I nodded my head at Mitch, letting him know to come on. We walked out of the room and closed the door behind us. One to go.

———

*P*ulling into Mitch's driveway I turned the car off and waited for him to get out. There were a lot of things going through my head and I didn't know how to handle it.

"How was Mya?" He questioned before getting out.

"She hurt but she is going to get better. She is pregnant *mano*." I blurted out shaking my head.

"What does that gotta do with you?"

I looked at him for a couple of seconds to let him think about it.

"Oh shit it's yours?" He asked looking at me.

"I think so. That's what she said." I confessed.

"How the fuck you let that happen?" He looked at me like I was crazy.

"I don't fucking know it just happened."

"Well what are you going to do *amigo*?" He questioned looking at me.

"I'm going to take care of what's mine. Believe me, but I feel bad about lying to her about her boyfriend. What do you think I should do?"

"First off fuck that nigga. You don't owe shit to that nigga. He obviously didn't want her and he handed her to you on a silver platter. For all she know he died in that car accident his dumb ass caused. Now you gotta step up and build her up. Mold her and don't change her make sure you got your shit together so y'all two can raise this kid y'all having. I know this shit happened faster than you thought and y'all not together but it's God's plan. Don't try to force her into a relationship with you, just be there for her and let her know that you are here for her. Let her heal." He stopped and the car was quiet for a second.

"That was the deepest shit you ever said." I spoke before I started laughing.

"Man fuck you. Let me get up out of here. I got a date tonight." He pushed me before opening his door.

"Who is it this time?" I questioned.

"Don't worry about me, worry about you." He laughed and closed the door and walked away.

I chuckled and beeped my horn twice before pulling out of the driveway. What he didn't know was that I knew who he was going out on a date with. I had overheard Aaliyah telling Kris all about it.

I headed to the hospital to see Mya. I hope she wasn't worried about having my baby. I knew I was going to be there for her whenever she needed me, that was one thing for sure.

. . .

*W*hen I walked into her room she was sitting up in her bed with her eyes glued to the tv and eating at the same time. She didn't know I was there until I knocked on the door. She looked over at me and smiled before muting the tv.

"What were you watching?" I grabbed a chair and sat down looking at her.

"Basketball wives." She answered simply before stuffing more food in her mouth.

"I never heard of that."

"What! How have you never heard of Basketball wives, this is like the best show ever." She looked at me surprised.

"I don't watch tv for real because I'm not always home." I shrugged my shoulders.

"Why is that?" She asked.

It was obvious that she didn't know that Damien was a part of the Valley boys, so I wasn't about to tell her what I actually did.

"I just be busy all the time."

"Well you are not busy right now so we are going to watch it together." She smiled and unmuted the tv and focused her attention back on it.

"How's your body? Are you feeling okay?" I inquired.

"I feel a little better now. My ankle on my broken leg hurts a little bit, and it hurts to laugh." She replied, shrugging her shoulders.

"Let me see if I can make it better." I grabbed her foot and started massaging it.

"How do you feel about me staying with you? You know I can stay at my own house." She smiled at me as I continued to massage her foot.

"I mean you can, but you won't have anybody there to help you until you get better."

"I guess you're right. I just don't want to be a burden to you." She admitted dropping her head.

"You are not a burden at all, and look I know that this probably not how you wanted it to be. Pregnant and not in a relationship, but I will be here every step of the way to help you through this. I need you to help me through this because this is all new to me.

Even though I didn't know if the baby was mine I was going to take care of her. She needed somebody here for her and that person was me. I wasn't going to let her go through this on her own.

Chapter Sixteen

MYA-1 WEEK LATER

"Is that everything?" I asked curiously as Pharaoh put boxes in my room.

I got out of the hospital four days ago and Pharaoh came to get me from the hospital. We had spent a couple of days packing up my house, well it was mostly him because he didn't want me moving around on my leg. Pharaoh has been the sweetest person to me. He treated me like I was a queen and made sure I was okay at all times. Even when he was out he would call every five minutes to make sure. I couldn't get too happy because Damein was the same way until he started beating me.

I was still sad that he died and I didn't get to say goodbye, but I was happy because I don't know how long I could have put up with him beating on me.

"No, I still have a couple more.¿*Tienes hambre (Are you*

hungry)?" He looked at me from the doorway. His eyes were so soft and full of concern.

"Am I hungry?" I inquired not knowing what he said.

"Si." He smiled and nodded his head.

"Yeah I thought you would never ask." I laughed and he shook his head.

"Closed mouths don't get fed, and stop doubting yourself you got it." He stated.

"What do you mean?"

"You know how to speak Spanish you 're just acting scary."

"No I don't." I spat.

"Then tell me what you want in spanish." He challenged me.

One thing I didn't do was back down from a challenge. Never did, and never will. I decided that this was the best way to fix how I was feeling. I thought for a second to get my sentence together and then I smiled.

"Te quiero (I want you)."

"¿Me quieres (You want me)?"

"Sí, muy malo (Yes, very bad)." I nodded my head and winked at him.

He smiled and started to slowly walk over to me.

"¿Està bien (Is that right)?"

I nodded my head again.

"Bien, muéstrame (Then, show me)!" He walked all the way up to me and caressed my cheek

I grabbed a hold of his pants so that his print was right in my face. I smiled up at him as I unzipped his jeans and pulled them down along with his briefs.

When his dick sprung out at attention it smacked me on the side of my face and I chuckled, before I wrapped my lips around his tip, slowly taking him into my mouth.

"Ooo, yeah just like that." Pharaoh hissed and grabbed the back of my head holding it in place as he started grinding in and out of my mouth.

I looked up at him to see what his facial expression looked like and he smiled down at me.

I continued to suck him dry until he took a step back and stroked himself as he licked his lips.

"Lay back for me *bebita*."

I slowly laid back on the bed and looked at him with lust in my eyes. I was tempted to pull him to me, but I just laid back like he said.

He looked at me as he stepped out of his jeans and took his shirt off. He stroked himself and walked up to the bed before reaching out and pulling my leggings down along with my panties. Once he got them off he ran his hand down the middle of my body until he got to my wet box.

Smiling at me, he inserted two of his fingers into me making me gasp and arch my back off of the bed. He continued to move his fingers in and out of me, never taking his eyes off of me. Before I knew it, he had dipped down and began to eat me out as he continued to finger me.

He licked, sucked, and nibbled on my pussy sending me over the top. I grabbed his head letting him know to go deeper, and he did just that. I grinded my hips on his face matching his pace before coming on his lips.

After he sucked up all of my juices he looked at me and positioned himself between my legs. I took my shirt and bra off and bit my bottom lip as he slowly entered me. As he pushed his way through it felt like he was stretching me out as he entered me, so I put my hand on his stomach trying to push him back.

"Move yo hand," He hissed before grabbing both of my hands and pinning them above my head. "You said you wanted this dick, so stop running from me and take it." He bent down and kissed me on my lips and pushed all the way in.

He began to speed up the pace, never letting my hands go. He was giving me what I wanted for sure. That's what I got for acting thirsty.

"Are you going to cum for me Mya?" He questioned softly looking me dead in my eyes.

His accent was so sexy and it made me want to cum as soon as he said it. When I was with Damien, he never really talked during sex. He would bust his nut and then fall asleep, but not with Pharaoh. I would cum multiple times before he came and it made me feel special. Usually I didn't do a lot of talking during sex, but Pharaoh made me want to try new things.

I nodded my head hoping that would count as a yes because I was finding it hard to speak.

"I can't hear you Mya. Are you going to cum for me." He

began to speed up his pace and I took my bottom lip into my mouth.

He felt so damn good and I wanted to grip something but I couldn't because Pharaoh still had my hands pinned above my head.

"I'm about to cum. Oh fuck!" I moaned out loudly.

"Cum for me Mya." He spoke, his accent was thick and strong sending me over the top.

My legs shook and I came all over Pharaoh's dicked before dropping my legs. For the first time in my life I was genuinely tired. I just wanted to roll over and sleep for the rest of the day.

"You good *bebita?*" Pharaoh pulled out of me and grabbed his boxers off of the floor.

He put them back on and then sat on the bed next to me. He rubbed my belly and I laid there just looking and thinking.

"Yes I'm okay, did you get to finish?" I questioned not remembering if he came or not.

"Nah I didn't but it ain't about me. You couldn't hang and I don't need to be pushing you." He chuckled and looked at me.

"I can hang." I argued, frowning at him.

"Yeah okay. Look, I'm about to go get something to eat. I'll be back in a little bit." He stood up and started putting his clothes back on before whistling.

A couple seconds later Chloe and Chaos came running into the room. When Chaos saw me he ran up and jumped on the bed, laying right next to me. Chloe on the other hand stood by Pharaoh just looking at me. Even though Chloe was a dog, she was still like Pharaoh's daughter and I know she felt like I was taking her spot in Pharaoh's life. I wasn't about to fight for attention with anybody or anything especially a dog.

"Y'all stay in here until I get back. Chloe fix your attitude." Pharaoh spoke sternly looking down at Chloe.

Once he left Chloe looked at me and then laid down on the floor closing her eyes. I looked over at Chaos and he looked at me, waiting for me to do something.

"At least you like me right." I asked Chaos and he started wagging his tail and trying to get me to pet him.

I started to rub him on the top of his head and he snuggled close to me. I pulled the covers over my naked body and drifted off to sleep.

Chapter Seventeen

PHARAOH

"You look nervous. You alright?" I asked Mya as her legs shook and she looked out the passenger side window.

We were on our way to dinner to meet our parents and tell them what was happening between Mya and I. I had to force Mya to tell her parents to meet us because she was scared of what they might think. I told her that I would be next to her the entire time and I would answer anything she didn't want to. We had to let all of our parents know that they will have a grandchild soon and this was the perfect way to do it. Even though this was everybody's first time meeting each other, hopefully everything will go smoothly.

"I just hope they don't ask a lot of questions." Mya confessed sighing.

"You already know they are going to ask questions, you

gotta be a big girl and handle it like a grown woman. Just look at it as you are in the courtroom on yo lawyer shit and you will be good."

I pulled into the parking lot of the restaurant I had reserved for the dinner and turned the car off.

Mya let out a deep breath and looked at me. I smiled and grabbed her hand.

"They are going to be alright and even if they are not then you still got me and we are going to get through this whether they do it or not." I reassured her, squeezing her hand lightly.

"I hope so."

"Me too, now come on let's go up in here and handle business." I smiled and got out of the car, walking over to her side and letting her out.

When we walked into the restaurant it was a little crowded, but that didn't matter because I rented out the upper half just for us and our parents. I let the hostess know who I was and she escorted us up the stairs to our table.

Once we got up the stairs, I saw my parents sitting at the table talking to each other. My parents meant the world to me and I would do anything for them. Even though they had no idea what I did for a living, they supported everything I did. Hopefully they would accept Mya and support us and our baby.

"MaMa y Pops." I called out to them once we got to the table.

They both looked between me and Mya and stood up smiling at us.

"¡*Hijo! ¿Cómo estás y quién es esta hermosa dama (Son! How are you and who is this pretty lady)?*" My momma asked looking Mya up and down with a smile.

"*Estoy bien mama* (I'm good mama), " I hugged my mom and dad before stepping back and putting my hand on the nape of Mya's back. "This is Mya. Mya, these are my parents, Eliza and Anthony Rivera."

Instead of my mom taking my dad's last name, my dad took hers to show her parents that he was really serious about marrying their daughter. My dad gave up a lot to be with my mom, but you would never know because he never complained about it.

"It's so nice to meet you both. I've heard so much about you two." Mya smiled and shook their hands.

"Well that's funny because we have heard very little about you." My mom gave me the stink eyes before sitting back down in her seat.

"Don't pester him Liza. He doesn't have to tell you about every girl that he dates." My dad jumped in taking up for me.

"Thank you pops, and mama you meeting her face to face that's better than me telling you about her. Now you got her here live and in person." I stated honestly.

Once we were all seated I grabbed Mya's hand under the table and she smiled at me before tucking her curly hair behind her ear.

"So what do y'all got us here for?" My dad asked curiously looking between me and Mya.

"Can we order our drinks first? We gotta wait on Mya's

parents to get here." I spoke and on cue two people, a man and a woman walked up to the table.

"Mya?" The lady spoke standing at the end of the table.

"Mom, dad hey." Mya quickly got up and hugged her parents before holding her hand out for mine.

I stood up and walked up to them and they both had a confused look on their face like something was wrong.

"I want you guys to meet Pharaoh Rivera. Pharaoh, these are my parents Terry and Rachel Sanders." She smiled and hooked her arm with mine, pulling me closer.

"Nice you meet you two." I smiled and stuck out my hand for them to shake but they stood there looking at it like it was dirty.

"Who is this and where is Damien?" Her mother asked, looking me up and down in disgust.

Mya took her arm out of mine and the smile she once had on her face had now disappeared. I looked at Mya and she just stood there with her head down. I knew that meant I would have to answer the question for her.

"He died about a month ago in a car accident." I spoke for Mya.

"Again who are you? Mya, you know how to talk, don't have this man who we never even met before talking for you. You are way too old for that shit." Her dad butted in.

I looked at her mom and then her dad, before looking down at her awaiting her response.

"This is my friend Pharaoh. Damien isn't here because he

died in a car accident he caused last month. He tried to kill me." She confessed.

"What did you do to make him want to go and do that?" Her mom questioned, making me look at her like she was crazy.

This whole conversation started to get weird and I was getting a bad feeling. Looking at her parents I knew exactly what the problem was.

I dropped my head and chuckled lightly to myself before lifting it back up to say something. They didn't know who I was, and I didn't but I was about to give them a lesson. I don't bite my tongue for nobody and I wasn't about to start now.

"The fuck is wrong with y'all two? Y'all only daughter just told y'all that her boyfriend wanted to kill her and all y'all got to say is what did she do to cause it? Are you serious right now? I know y'all seen the bruises and shit cause it wasn't that hard for me to see them. He beat her every chance he got and she ain't do shit for two years while he beat her ass for nothing. This y'all daughter y'all supposed to be on her side. Terry I want you to hear me clearly when I say this. Any man who has to beat his wife or girlfriend to show their dominance, is not a man at all. A father should protect their children and let no harm come to them. You sat back while another man beat your daughter, not lifting a finger or saying a word. You are a coward to me. We called y'all here out of respect, but y'all don't deserve to hear shit we have to say. Rachel I hope one day you open your eyes like your daughter did and see that you deserve better than what you are getting. Terry, you are a sorry excuse for a father, husband, and human being, I hope you die slow." I looked between the two of them and their facial expressions were priceless.

I had never disrespected anybody's parents before, but Mya's father deserved every word that I said. I hadn't heard Mya say anything and at this point I didn't care if she was mad or not. I spoke my mind and I didn't feel bad at all.

"Mom. Dad. I think you should go." Mya stated speaking up.

Her parents looked between the both of us and when they saw that neither one of us was budging, they scuffed, turned around, and walked away.

Once they were gone I wrapped Mya in my arms and she began to cry.

"Don't cry *bebita*. Everything will be alright. *Mi familia es su familia (My family is your family.*" I reassured her by letting her know that me and my family had her.

Finally getting her to calm down, we walked back over to the table and sat down. My parents just looked at us with sympathy.

"*Disculpa por lo que le sucedió a tu hija.*" My momma said breaking the silence.

My mom was bilingual like me, but most of the time she spoke spanish.

"She said she is sorry what happened to you daughter." I translated for her, as she spoke to Mya.

"*Uh. Gracias. Es triste pero lo tengo Pharaoh aquí para ayudar.*

(Uh. Thank you. It's sad but I have Pharaoh here to help) " Mya smiled up at me and lightly tapped my thigh under the table.

"¿Oh Ella habla español (Oh she speaks spanish)?" My momma asked, surprised.

"Si, un poco (Yes, a little). I'm teaching her." I responded

"Enough with all the talking, what did you really call us here for son?" My dad interjected.

"Well since you are so impatient. Mya and I are having a baby." I smiled, not wanting the secrecy to go on any longer.

My mom quickly put her hands on her mouth and stood up out of her chair.

"Felicitaciones!" She shouted rushing over to our side of the table to hug us.

I knew my family was going to be excited and welcoming since Mya was the only woman to ever meet my parents to begin with. Mya was going to enjoy this new family of hers.

Chapter Eighteen

MYA

$\mathcal{I}$ was sitting down on instagram laughing at the funny videos on my explore page, while the nail tech went to work on my nails. I hadn't been to get my nails done in a while because Damien didn't like them, but I wanted to feel pretty again.

I told Aaliyah and Kris to meet me, so we could talk and catch up. I really have been waiting to tell them what went down when me and Pharaoh told our parents that we were having a baby. I hadn't talked to my parents since that day. I wasn't planning on it either.

They didn't have my back at all. They took Damien's side like they always did. They made it seem like Damirn was their kid and not me. I haven't told anybody about my mom getting abused by my dad because it was none of their business. My mom hid it so well. At least I thought she did until Pharaoh pointed it out. My dad never laid a finger on her when I was watching, and it was always done in the privacy of their room. He would always say that he had to hit my mom to teach her lesson because if he didn't she wouldn't know how to act.

"Well I'll be damned. Look Aaliyah she is alive." Kris knocked me out of my thoughts as him and Aaliyah walked through the doors of the nail salon.

I haven't seen them since I had gotten out of the hospital a couple of weeks ago. I was so busy trying to pack up and move in with Pharaoh. Plus I had to heal from all of my injuries I sustained in the car accident.

"Yeah I thought Damien found her and killed her for good this time." Aaliyah sucked her teeth as she sighed at the clipboard.

"What do you mean? Damien is dead." I looked at her puzzled.

"Excuse me sweetheart heart he is not dead." Kris corrected me.

"What do you mean he's not dead? Pharaoh said that he was dead." I looked between the both of them.

I was hoping they were lying to me.

"The hospital never released him, and when we asked the doctor what he died from he told us that Damien checked himself out." Aaliyah confessed, sitting down in the waiting chair.

"Pharaoh told me that he died." I repeated myself.

I wanted to believe that he was dead, but if he wasn't where was he? Why did Pharaoh tell me that he was dead?

"If he was dead then where is his body?" Aaliyah questioned looking between me and Kris

"Exactly, I haven't seen an obituary, a funeral, or even ashes for the nigga and Pharaoh probably told you that so you wouldn't be scared." Kris added in making me scared.

"I have to tell Pharaoh, what if he knows where I am." I was starting to get paranoid.

"You can tell him, but it's not going to matter anyway because Pharaoh knows how to handle himself. Trust and believe that." Kris stated, sure of himself.

I thought about it for a second and then reassured myself that I was okay with Pharaoh around. I knew that he wouldn't let Damien near me ever again.

"I guess you're right," I said, relaxing .

I texted Pharaoh letting him know that I would be home in a couple of hours and we had to talk. He quickly responded by saying he would be there by the time I got home.

"I know I am. Now what do you want me to do with your hair?" He questioned catching me off guard.

"Who said I wanted you touching my hair?" I asked him a stank face.

"Oh no bitch don't do that. You know I'm the only one that can tame that mess you call hair." He yelled, making me and Aaliyah bust out laughing.

"Stop your moving!" The nail tech demanded making me freeze and chuckle.

"I'm sorry." I apologized, shaking my head.

"It's okay but don't get angry when your nails do not come out right." She spoke sternly before continuing in my nails.

After about ten minutes my nails were done and it looked like I actually took care of myself. I waited until Kris and Aaliyah were finished and then we all went to Kris house so that he could do my hair.

I was leaving Kris's house and headed home to talk to Pharaoh when my phone started ringing. I reached over and grabbed it out of my purse to see that it was Jessica calling. I quickly answered it and put it to my ear.

"Hey Jessica what's up."

"Hey please tell me that you're okay to come back to work today." She sounded stressed and annoyed at the same time.

I never knew Jessica could be a person who stressed about anything. She always had everything under control, so something must have been serious.

"What's wrong?" I questioned my concern.

"This temp is driving me up the walls. Everything is late getting filed, there's things being put in the wrong places. Basically everything is going wrong, and there's a guy by the name of Tyrone Waverly who has been coming in everyday the past month and I half looking for you." She confessed, making me feel bad.

"Do you know why? I was surprised.

"Nope all he told me was you were one of the best in the city and he only wanted to speak to you. He is here now by the way. Can I tell him that you are on your way?" She questioned hopeful.

"Sure Jess I'll be there and you have to come out with me this weekend." I smiled hoping she would say yes.

Jessica wasn't the going out type. She was always busy with cases and everything else that was going on in her life. She barely had any time to herself.

"If you come back permanently until you have your baby, I'll be happy to."

"Great your my date. I will pick you up Saturday night. I'll tell you more as the week goes by."

"Okay, please hurry and can you please bring me something to eat. This temp isn't feeding me either." She whined.

"Sure, you want your usual?"

"Yes, please."

"Okay I'll be there in an hour." I chuckled before hanging up the phone as I continued down the street.

Luckily my job was in the same direction I was going, so I didn't have to turn around.

———

"*O*h my god, Mya you are a lifesaver." Jessica exclaimed excitedly as I walked into her office with her food.

She quickly got up out of the chair and walked up to me retrieving her food.

"You're welcome, and I already told the temp that he could go home."

"Thank god, and Mr. Waverly is patiently waiting in your office waiting to speak with you. Go see what that man wants, he has waited long enough." She shooed me away.

I laughed and then turned around walking to my office. When I walked through the door, Tyrone's back was turned to me as he sat waiting in one of the chairs I had in front of my desk.

"Hi, Mr. Waverly, my name is Mya. I heard that you have been looking for me." I spoke, making him turn around and look at me.

When he saw that it was really me he smiled and slowly walked over to me.

"Mya Sanders. I really thought Damien made you all up. You look way better than what he described you to look like. No wonder he never brought you around." He spoke softly sending chills down my spine.

This man was fine. His smooth chocolate skin made me want to take a bite out of him and his freshly cut beard and hair top off his looks. His waves were on swim and the tailored suit he had on fit perfectly. It looked like he had just stepped off the cover of a magazine. His looks almost made me forget what he had said a couple of seconds earlier.

"You know Damien?" I questioned.

"Yeah I know Damien." He answered simply smiling at me.

I hoped and prayed Damien didn't send him here to scare me.

"How? Are you two friends?" I asked curiously.

"Me and Damien are...business partners. I don't use the term friends lightly, but I'm not here to discuss who I associate myself with. See business partners make money together and Damien recently came up on a whole lot of money and didn't cut me in. Now he is nowhere to be found, I was hoping you could tell me where I could find him." He asked.

His once smooth and calming voice was now filled with bitterness.

I had no idea what money he was talking about and how Damien even played a role in all of this. Damien never told me about coming up on anything let alone money so wasn't going to be much of a help.

"Missing? Tyrone, Damien is dead. He died in a car accident a month and a half ago. As for any money, he never told me about it so I'm not sure what you are talking about." I confessed to him.

"Are you lying to me Mya, because I have been looking for him over a month now and I can't seem to find him or his body. So something isn't adding up." He walked up to me and caressed my cheek smiling at me. "I wouldn't want you dying because you are not telling me the truth."

At that moment I was scared of Tyrone. I had know idea who he was and what he and Damien had going on, but he scared me.

"I'm not lying to you." I shivered and he pulled me closer to him.

"You're not scared of me are you Mya?" He questioned with a smirk on his face.

I shook my head lying.

He ran his hand down my back until he got to the nape of my back. He smiled at me and leaned closer like he was going to kiss me. Instead he leaned forward some more until I could feel his breath on my ear.

"You should be." He took a step back and fixed his suit before walking to the door of my office and looking back at me. "I'll be in touch Mya." He winked and then walked out of my office, closing the door behind him.

I was lost because on one hand this man was fine, but on the other hand I knew it was the devil dressed in Louie V.

Chapter Nineteen

PHARAOH

"**G**o ahead tell him what you told me." I spoke to Mya as her, Mitch and I sat in my living room.

Chloe and Chaos laid by my feet as we talked about what had Mya so scared today.

"I was on my way home when Jessica called and told me that there was a man there who had been coming up to my job asking for me ever since Damien died. His name is Tyrone Waverly. When I got there he told me that him and Damien were business partners and Damien went missing. He said Damien came up with some money and didn't cut him in. Now he's looking for it and he is going to keep coming for me until he gets it. The thing is I don't know what he is talking about. Damein never told me about coming into some money." From the look on her face she was scared.

"Mya can you take them out for me while I talk to Mitch

for a second." I asked through clenched teeth and a smile on my face.

"Yeah, come on Chloe and Chaos." She spoke before whistling.

They both got up and raced each other out of the living room, making Mya laugh and walk out of the room. Once I heard the back door close I looked at Mitch who was staring off into space.

"So you mean to tell me that nigga Damien played us?" Mitch semi yelled, making me shush him.

"Why are you so loud my nigga!"

"My bad so what are you going to do, find out where he hid the money?" Mitch inquired.

"Exactly. I'm going to need Tyrone distracted. Then I'll kill him and get my money back." I stated simply shrugging my shoulders.

"Well he doesn't know where it is and neither does Mya."

"Damien was a very good liar. He fooled us into believing that he didn't have my money. Maybe he doesn't have my money because he gave it to somebody else."

"Who does he know other than Mya and the niggas he hang with."

"See that's where you come in at. He has to have some-body who he is giving his money to and you are going to find that out. In the meantime we are going to let Tyrone believe that Mya has it." I explained to him.

"Why though. What are you getting out of this?'"

"I got him just where I want him. Close. We need to keep

him occupied and distracted with Mya. Once I find out where my money is, he will be as good as dead. Plus we don't need Mya finding out what really happened to Damien."

"So you plan on lying to her about him until when?"

"I'm not lying to her. He's dead." Before I could finish my sentence, Chloe and Chaos ran into the living room.

That meant Mya was close behind.

"Find out where my money is Mitch" I whispered just as Mya walked in the room with a smile on her face.

"I'll call you if I find anything. See you later Mya." Mitch smiled before he disappeared around the corner.

I sighed and sat down on the couch with my head in my hands. Even though Mya had nothing to do with what was going on and I didn't want her to be in it, I couldn't help but know that she was right in the middle of everything. I was ready to kill any and everybody who had my money Nate got robbed and killed for. Even if they had no idea. Tyrone used to work with us when we first started this, but then he felt like he wasn't making enough and left to hang with the Valley boys. He knew not to come back this way. He must not have known that Mya was with a boss now, but soon he will find out. They didn't show Nate any remorse when they killed him, and I was going to return the favor.

"Hey you okay?" Mya questioned making me lift my head up and look at her.

I had forgotten that she had even come back into the room.

"Yeah I'm alright *bebita* just thinking about some shit.

Come here for a second." I held my hand out for her and she walked over to me smiling.

Once she grabbed my hand I pulled her down onto my lap, before rubbing my hand on her belly in a circular motion. She wasn't showing yet, but she was starting to get a bump.

"How are you feeling?" I asked, looking her in the eyes as she stared me back in mine.

"I'm scared. What if Damien is out there? He already tried to kill me once, and if he finds out this baby isn't his he will really try to kill me and our baby. What if he's the one who sent Tyrone after me." She rattled off with a scared look on her face.

"Hey look at me," I cupped her chin and made her look at me again.

"Damien is dead. I promise you that he can't hurt you anymore." I wiped the lone tear that fell from her eye. "Nobody will ever hurt you again. I promise." I spoke honestly and from the heart.

I didn't want her to hurt ever again.

"Why me? Why do you want to be with me?"

"Because you are a beautiful, smart, and head strong woman who fell in love with the wrong person. I want you to see how much of a blessing you are. Believe it or not I need you here more than you need me." I caressed her face, making her smile.

I meant every word from the bottom of my heart. I didn't want her to ever hurt again, but I knew if she ever found out about what really happened to Damiwn she would hate me.

Hopefully I found my money and killed Tyrone before she ever found out. For right now I was going to show her all of the love and attention she needed.

"I think I'm falling for you Pharaoh." She looked me dead in my eyes so I knew she was telling the truth.

"You should go take a shower and get dressed in something cute. I have to go make a run and then I swing back around here and take you out. I want you to enjoy your pregnancy and that means going out and having fun. I want to show you off." I smiled ignoring what she said. I kissed her lips before tapping her on the thigh to let her know to get up.

"Are you not going to come back and get dressed with me?" She questioned.

I looked down at my blue Balmain Jeans and plain white Bathing Ape t-shirt confused. I thought what I had on was cool.

"Nah, but I'll be back though." I kissed her lips and then turned around walking out of the house.

---

*T*o make sure all of my workers obeyed me, I had to show some tough love. That meant I had to put my foot down to let them know not to cross me.

I had to go find Cameron. He was one of the dudes who was supposed to be with Nate when he got killed. After Nate was killed Cameron went MIA, and it made me believe that he had something to do with Nate getting robbed. I got my answer when I killed the first *vato* who had something to do with it. I had people out looking for him and when they told me that he had been staying in a hotel, I made it my mission to pay him a little visit.

I was sitting on the bed of his hotel room when the door unlocked and he walked with a girl laughing. The light was off so he couldn't see me, but I could see him. When he turned the light on and saw me sitting there he stopped in his tracks.

"Rebecca you should go, I'll call you tomorrow." He spoke to the girl next to him, never taking his eyes off of me.

The girl just stood there not moving, making me irritated.

"Either you leave now or I'll take this 9 I got in my pants out, and you leave when the EMT's roll you out on a gurney." I spoke nicely as I smiled at her.

I could tell she was confused and scared because she kept looking at Cameron for help. He just told her to go.

Once she left, I walked over to the door closing and locking it before turning back to Cameron.

"What are you doing here Ro. How did you find me?" He had the nerve to ask, pissing me off more.

I was going to wait but I couldn't. I quickly pulled out my 9mm and shot him once I'm both of his knees sending him crying to the floor.

"You don't get to ask me no fucking questions you pussy ass nigga. You got Nate killed because only you and him knew where the money was. Ain't no way you were the only one that made it out that trap alive if you ain't sell him out. So answer this Cameron, what did you get out of it?"

"They told me if I helped them they would give me some of the money and I could get out of the game and leave town. Only problem was that Damien took both me and Tyrone's cut for himself." He explained after he caught his breath.

"So you did all of this shit because you ain't want to sell no more?"

He nodded his head and I laughed.

"Funny thing about that is that you don't get to just leave, but you make your decision. You want out." I held my gun and emptied my clip. "You're free to go." I tucked my gun back into my waistband and left the room.

Instead of taking the elevator and going through the front doors of the hotel, I took the stairs and out of the back doors.

MYA

I almost tripped in my heels three times as Pharaoh led me to wherever he was taking me. I couldn't see because he had me blindfolded, but he held my waist to guide me.

"Pharaoh where are we going?" I whined

"How many times are you going to ask me that? I'm not telling you, now just keep walking we are almost there." He laughed and continued to guide me.

We walked for a little while longer and then he told me that we were about to go up some stairs so be careful. Once we finished walking up the stairs, I was told to sit down and remove the blindfold. When I removed the blindfold I saw that we were on a private jet. I looked around in amazement, before looking at Pharaoh who stood up smiling down at me.

"Let me go tell the pilot that we are ready to go, you make yourself comfortable."

He walked away and I stood up and walked around to see what the private jet had in store. I walked to the back of the jet where the cabinets were and opened one to find it full of snacks. I smiled when I saw a pack of chocolate chip cookies. I quickly grabbed it out of the cabinet and opened it. I was so focused out eating the cookies that I didn't notice Pharaoh standing behind me. I turned around to see him trying to hold onto his laughter.

"I see you found the snack cabinet." He chuckled and walked up to me taking a cookie out of the pack.

"This is your jet?" I asked, amazed.

If it was his I knew it cost a pretty penny, so I was trying to figure out what he did for a living to make enough money to buy him a private jet.

"Yeah, I don't take it up too often but it's mine. Come on we should sit down, the pilot is getting ready to take off." He grabbed my hand and we walked over to the seats to sit down.

I was scared and nervous to say the least. I had never been on an airplane let alone a jet and I was trying to act normal. The jet started to move and I gripped the leather seat for dear life.

"*Bebita* are you scared?" Pharaoh asked, placing his hand on top of mine.

"Yes. I've never been on a plane before." I chuckled nervously.

"We haven't taken off yet, you want me to go tell him to stop? He tried to get up but I stopped him.

"No, no it's okay. I will have to face my fears someday." I calmly said, making him sit back down.

The jet started to speed up down the runway, and my heartbeat started to speed up. I was starting to shake and hyperventilate and Pharaoh grabbed my hand. He put the armrest up that separated the seats up and then started to take off his belt.

"Lift that dress up, take them panties off and come hop on this dick. I'm about to show you how good it feels to fly on a jet." He smiled and pulled his pants down to his ankles.

I smiled and stood up and removed my panties just like he said. The plane was speeding down the runway so fast that my legs were starting to shake.

"You better hurry up and climb on board." He smirked and stroked himself as he waited for me.

I quickly lifted my dress up and climbed up on the chair. He took his hands off his dick and held onto my waist as I slowly slid all the way down on him. I gasped as the plane went up into the air. I looked out of one of the windows as we got higher and higher off the ground. I was busy watching the plane go up so Pharaoh started thrusted his hips upwards making me hold onto his shoulders.

"Look at me, don't worry about what's going on outside just focus on me." He spoke softly, making me look down at him.

He smiled up at me and then took his bottom lip into his mouth as he started speeding his pace up. I threw my head back as he held me in place. He felt so good going in and out of me, so I started moaning his name. I couldn't let him do all of the work so I made sure my heels were firmly on the seat and started to bounce on his dick.

"Look at you. Facing your fears *Bebita.* Yeah bounce just like that." He snarled and slapped me on the ass making me hiss.

"I'm about to come." I screamed out.

"¡*Venga(Come on)!* I'm right behind you." He gripped my waist tight as I came all over his dick.

I wrapped my arms around his neck and laid my head on his shoulders. I was exhausted so I closed my eyes and steadied my breath.

"I'm not afraid to fly in a plane anymore." I laughed, breaking the silence.

"I figured that much. We have an hour and a half until we land so you can sleep if you are tired.

He didn't have to tell me twice I was already dozing off as he finished his sentence.

———

My eyes fluttered open, and I expected Pharaoh to be under me like he was when I fell asleep but he wasn't. Instead I was in the backseat of a car and I had no idea where I was. My first thought was how in the world did he get me from the plane to the car and the next thought was where was he. I sat up in the car and rubbed my eyes before I noticed a man standing outside of the driver side smoking a cigarette.

I was about to ask him where I was when I heard a door open. I look over to Pharaoh getting in with bags in his hands.

"I'm in Las Vegas for the night, keep an eye on them until I get back. She needed some time away from LA, but look she woke now, so I'm going to get at you later. Hit me back if anything changes." He hung up the phone and smiled at me before closing the door.

"Well look who decided to wake up. How'd you sleep love." He questioned

"Pretty good. Quick question though. How did I get from the airport to the car and who is that man?" I asked, pointing to the man outside.

"He's our driver for the day and I carried you. Even though I thought you would wake up way before then. I tire you out quickly." He smirked and licked his lips.

"Don't flatter yourself, this kid of yours makes me tired. You just finish me off."

"I'll take that. Here I bought you a little something to put on when we get to the room. I got a couple things planned for us." He handed me the bag and I looked inside to see a swimsuit.

When we got to what looked like a beach house we rushed in to change. I hoped he got the right size but instead of saying anything I walked into the room to put it on. After I finished getting dressed I looked at myself in the mirror and walked out of the room to see Pharaoh in swim trunks drinking henny straight from the bottle.

"Damn blue looks good on you. Are you ready to go?" He asked me before putting the bottle down.

"Yes I'm ready, where did you get a bottle of henny from?." I smiled and walked up to him.

"The cabinet. Come on let's go."

He grabbed my hand and we walked out of the room and then around the back of the room to a set of glass doors that led to a beach. When my feet hit the sand I smiled as it got between my toes. I haven't been to the beach since I was a kid, so being able to go to one now brought back the kid in me.

"What are you thinking about?" He questioned breaking bone out of my thoughts.

"It's just that I haven't been to the beach since I was a kid and it's just bringing back a lot of memories." I laid my head on his bare shoulder as we walked to the shore line.

"You ready to make some new memories tonight?"

"Yeah, anything I do with you, I'll remember forever."

"Well I wanted to wait until after dinner but I think this is the right time."

"Right time for what?"

Pharaoh stopped walking and stood in front of me grabbing both of my hands.

"So I know these past couple of months have been a little crazy and we didn't meet on good terms, but I know you have been hurt a lot in your past relationship. You need somebody in your life who wouldn't harm a hair on your head and I need someone like you to hold me down. What I'm trying to say is,

Mya can you make it official and be my girl?" He smiled and caressed my cheek.

"You sure are making it hard for me to say no."

"Why would you say no?" He asked, taken back.

"I'm just playing, of course I'll be your girl."

He smiled again before hugging me and then kissing me. Hopefully this will be better than my last.

Chapter Twenty

PHARAOH

I woke up and looked around for a second and as I thought about the night I had with Mya. It started with a walk on the beach to get our feet wet, but then Mya wanted to get in the water. Her wish was my command last night. She got whatever she asked for. I had a candlelight dinner set up for her. Then when we made it back to the room I gave her this dick for dessert.

I looked over at the clock on the nightstand and it read twelve-thirty. I looked to the side of me to see Mya not there. I slid the covers off my body and got up out of the bed. I walked over to the dresser on the other side of the room and grabbed a pair of boxers, pulling them on.

I opened the door to my room and the smell of bacon and maple sausage hit my nose. I followed the sweet smell to the kitchen to see Mya standing at the stove in just her bra and panties. She was singing along to *Angel of Mine by Monica* and swaying back and forth. I didn't want to interrupt her because she sounded good harmonizing with Monica. Once the song was over I started clapping and she jumped and turned around.

"Pharaoh you scared me." She gasped and paused the music she was listening to.

"My bad, what's all off this?" I laughed and looked over at everything she had already set up.

There were eggs,grits, muffins, pancakes, homestyle potatoes, and fruit. I grabbed a strawberry and sat back down on the bar stool. Mya really made herself at home.

"This is a thank you for one of the best dates of my life." She walked up to the counter and leaned on it.

"Oh forreal? This is what I get for breaking your back in?" I smirked and reached across and grabbed another strawberry

Mya flipped the bacon and sausages before turning back to me.

"Yeah something like that." She chuckled.

"That's cool, I'm going to enjoy making everyday your best day with me." I fed her the strawberry and licked my lips as she bit into it.

"I'm glad you can do that. How did you sleep?" She asked pulling away to take the food off the stove.

"Good next to you. I was out like a light."

"I tire you out quickly." She joked, stealing my line.

"Yeah you do actually. Fucked up my sleep pattern. I don't ever wake up this late. I spoke, shaking my head.

"That's what I do." She popped her invisible collar making me laugh.

"Come on man and make our plates before you starve my baby." I waved her off and we laughed.

She made our plates and then she sat next to me. We talked and ate until our plates were cleaned and then we got dressed before heading back to California.

———

"*A*re you sure about this?" I questioned looking over at Mitch.

We were sitting outside of an old house looking at a lady and her son unload groceries and put them in the house. Mitch had told me that he found the person Damien gave the money he stole from me to.

"Yes I'm sure you told me to find out where he tucked the money and there you go." He exclaimed pointing out the passenger side window.

"So you telling me he had a whole six year old son and Mya ain't know nothing about it." I questioned.

"I'm saying we should talk to the lady first before we start shooting and killing people." He stated honestly pointing to the lady who got out of the car.

"Talk to her for what?"

"We gotta find out where she got the money, you don't know if she even got it in there."

"Nigga I thought you knew where it was at." I semi yelled in irritation.

"No my nigga. You told me to find out who he gave the money to. I did, there she go, so come on let's go talk to her." He smiled before getting out of the car and walking over to her.

I shook my head for a second. I didn't really need my money back because I had plenty more where that came from. It was the principal, plus I wanted everybody to know who ran LA. I wanted niggas to know that you never catch me or my niggas lacking and get away with it. If a couple innocent people get hurt in the process, then it's on the people they chose to hang out with.

"Excuse me, can we talk to you for a minute." I smiled as we walked up to the lady getting bags out of the car.

"Uh yeah, who are you?" She questioned.

She was a pretty dark skinned lady about five five and she was thick. I could see why Damienn liked her.

"We are some old friends of Damien, we wanted to talk to you for a second." Mitch answered looking over at me.

"I'm Camille. Is he okay? I haven't seen him in a while, he hasn't been home or came by to see his son." She exclaimed, sighing.

"Son? I didn't know Damien had a son." I spoke, genuinely surprised.

"Yeah he does. There he goes right here. DJ come here

meet some of your Daddy's friends." She waved him over as he made his way out of the house.

He looked to be six and he was a spitting image of Damien. I chuckled out loud before clearing my throat. I thought my secrets were bad. This nigga had secret lives and kids Mya didn't even know about.

"So you and Damien were together?" I was interested in where this conversation was going.

"Yes we've been together for three years. We used to be together in highschool, but we broke up and he started going with this girl named Mya. I got pregnant with DJ the summer I graduated from high school. Damien and Mya were taking a break and I was there for Damien. We lost communication for a couple years and once he found out DJ was his we got back together." She smiled as she reminisced about the past.

Too bad I was there to ruin the moment and turn that pretty little smile and her world upside down if she didn't have what I needed.

"See now that's a funny story because not only was Damien still with you behind Mya's back, he was with Mya behind your back. Judging by the look of surprise on your face, you didn't know that he died a couple months ago because he couldn't control his temper or keep his hands off things he knew he was not supposed to touch." I smiled and stepped closer to her.

The mixed look of terror and confusion on her face made my day. I reached up and tried to caress her cheek, but she took a step back holding onto her son in the process.

"Maybe you two should go." She spoke calmly and I almost thought she was scared anymore.

"Maybe we should. What do you think, Mano should we leave?" I asked looking back at Mitch.

"Not just yet." He answered.

"See *chiquita,* I know that Damien came up on a little money he stole from me before he died. Right before he died he told me that he didn't get a cut, and come to find out, he lied. Not only did he take his cut, he took somebody else's cut with him. That's where you and Junior come in. When I found out that he lied and Mya didn't have the money, I figured he gave it to somebody closer. Who better to give it to then his secret babymama and his secret kid. Now it's been a minute since he gave you the money so I'm pretty sure you spent some. I don't care about that. I want you to call this number when you have the rest of my money and I'll tell you what to do from there." I grabbed her phone from her hand and put my number in it before handing it back.

"When do you want it by?" She questioned her voice shaking from terror.

"I'll give you until the end of the week. Do you know anybody by the name of Tyrone Waverly?" I asked hopeful.

"Yeah that's DJ's godfather. Why?"

"I want you to deliver a message for me." I smiled and grabbed my 9mm pistol from my waist band and aimed it at Camille knee and pulled the trigger. She screamed out in pain as she fell to the ground.

"Let him know that he's next time he threatens or comes

near my girl he is dead, and when I see him he is dead." I smiled and turned around as Mitch followed behind me. "I'll see you Sunday night *chiquita*, that gives you a couple days to recuperate ." I threw over my shoulder as we walked to the car.

"Okay Jessica I have your sausage egg and cheese croissant, plus your espresso double shot latte with extra cream." I spoke walking into her office with the biggest smile on my face.

The day I spent with Pharaoh was the best. He treated me like a queen and he made me face my fears. I felt I could fly all over again. He made me feel like I was in good hands when he was around. I felt special.

"Well well well look who's all bright eyed and bushy tailed. How was your day with Prince Charming?" She asked, grabbing her food from my hand.

"It was amazing, he took me on his private jet to his beach house in Vegas. We had dinner on the beach and he asked me to be his girlfriend." I squealed in excitement.

"That's amazing. That's what you need after everything that you have been through. One thing of advice for you is to be aware and keep your eyes open. Don't let the lust you feel for him blind you from anything. You are about two and a half months pregnant and you and six more to go. You are going to be a mother soon so you have to be aware." She stated honestly before biting into her sandwich.

"I will Jessica."

"Alright now, there is a lady in your office she didn't give me a name but she said she was a friend from high school so I told her to wait for you there. I'll be heading out in thirty minutes to interview another client and I need that report for the Simmons case on my desk by the time you leave today." She demanded.

"You got it. I'll see you later." I nodded my head and walked out of her office.

Walking into my office, I was surprised to see Camille Hawkins sitting in a wheelchair in front of my desk. When I got closer she sniffled and turned around to face me. When our eyes met she broke down.

"Camille? What are you doing here and what happened to you?" I walked to get a better look at her.

Her leg was amputated at the knee and wrapped in bandages. I sat down and waited for her to talk in anticipation. She wiped her tears and calmed herself down before she started talking.

"First off I want to start off by saying that I didn't know

that you and Damien were together, but me and him have a son together. I found out I was pregnant the summer I graduated and then when I finally got a hold of Damien and told him he had a son he was all for taking care of him. We got back together about two years ago and he had been taking care of his son until he disappeared a couple months ago. Two men came to my house the other day. They told me that I had until Sunday night to give them the money that Damien stole from them. They said that Damien was dead and they seemed to know you. I came by to tell you to watch out. I can't give you a name because they didn't give me one, but he was Latino and he had an accent. He shot me in my leg in front of my son and didn't flinch or have a care in the world. Be careful." She spoke as the tears continued to roll down her face.

I sat there in disbelief as she talked. I was confused and angry at the same time. Not only was Damien cheating on me, he had a whole other family that I didn't know about. I was also angry because I knew exactly who she was referring to when she said a Latino man shot her..

"Thank you Camille so much for warning me, I'm sorry about your leg and what happened to you , but I have a couple of things I have to work on before I leave today. You can come by and talk whenever you need to." I was trying to rush her out so I could finish my paperwork and go home.

Camille got up and left and the smile on my face disappeared. I was pissed to say least and I was going to get to the bottom of all of this. I was done with the lies, secrets and bullshit. I needed to know who I was really dealing with. I didn't need a baby being brought into this world if it meant their life was in danger because of who their father was.

———

J was almost finished packing my last suitcase when Pharaoh came walking into the room. The smile he had in his face disappeared when he saw what I was doing. I was trying to hurry and pack before he came home but I had too many clothes for that.

"*¿Bebita qué pasa (baby girl what's up)?* Why are you packing?" He questioned walking up to me.

"I'm leaving. I can't stay here." I spoke not looking at him.

I was trying to keep the tears at bay, but they were trying the best they could to come out.

"Mya turn around and talk to me. What's wrong with you?" He asked, grabbing my arm and turning me around.

When I faced him I pulled away from him and wiped the tears that were falling from my eyes.

"You are the problem! You walk around here like you're this loving and genuine person fooling everybody, even your parents, but on the inside you're an evil soul!" I yelled, making him look at me crazy.

"Woah, where is all this animosity coming from?" He asked, taken back.

"I'm going to ask you this one time and I want the honest answer." I stated sternly.

"Alright what's up?" He asked egar.

"When you and Mitch left here when we got back from Las Vegas, you said that you were going out to handle some business. Did you or did you not go out and shoot an innocent woman in front of her son?" I looked at him and the expression on his face told it all.

"I did but-" He tried to justify himself but I held my hand up to stop him.

"You can't justify doing that Pharaoh, you can't. Do you not understand that we have a baby on the way? That woman is an innocent bystander like I am. She doesn't know what's going on. She is in the same boat with me. To do it in broad daylight in front of her son is just distasteful. There is no justifying that. You are a cold heartless person, and that's somebody I can't be with. I'm leaving today and don't try to stop me. I'll call you and tell you when the next doctor's appointment." I turned around and zipped my last suitcase up wiping the tears away that fell.

"Come on *bebita* you don't have to go. We can get through this. We can make it right." He begged, grabbing my forearm and turning me back to him.

"Us making it right is not going to my lady leg grow back and it is not going to erase those images from that little boy's brain. You need to find your heart and soul because anybody with either one of those, wouldn't have done what you did. It makes me wonder how many other people you have shot, injured or killed. Today I found out that the man I thought I would marry had a whole girlfriend and kid that

I didn't even know about. I'm done with the secrets and lies. I'm done."

I shook my head and walked around him grabbing my other suitcases. I looked back at him one last time before walking out of the room. I carried my suitcases down the stairs to the car. As I was putting the bags in the trunk Pharaoh came outside and walked up to me. When he got close enough it looked like he had been crying because his eyes were bloodshot. I couldn't give in so I looked away and continued to pack my car.

"Look Mya I know you have made up your mind but I couldn't let you leave without letting you know howPop I feel about you. You are an amazing, beautiful, intelligent woman and in a short period of time you have made me see what it's like to actually settle down and be with somebody for the rest of my life. You are a kindred spirit and that's what I have been looking for all my life. There is still a lot that I have done and a lot that I will do that you might not understand. In due time you will know that everything I do is for a reason. If you have to go figure out everything for a while I understand that and I'm not going to stop you. I just want you to know that you forever got my heart and my door is always open to you. Also, I don't want you stressing and shit like that so I want you to take these," He handed me a set of keys. "Those are the keys to my condo in downtown LA. I'll text you the address. It's closer to your job and I'm here whenever you need me. *Te amo bebita (I love you babygirl).*" He leaned forward and kissed me on my forehead before pulling back and caressing my cheek.

When he said that he loved me it broke my heart because even though I love him back, I couldn't get past the fact that he shot that lady in her leg in front of her son. It was going to take some time for me to forgive him. Time is what I needed. I needed time to be alone by myself for a while. I needed time to figure me out.

Chapter Twenty-Two

PHARAOH

"*A*we damn so she just broke up with you and left. Packed up all of her shit and bounced on yo stupid ass huh?" Mitch asked, chuckling.

We were at the strip club and as the strippers stripped in front of me, all I could think about was Mya. I wanted to come here to get my mind off of her but I couldn't. I was going to give her the space she needed, but I wasn't planning on letting her go in the process. I was going to be there whenever she needed me since that was all I could do for now.

"I'm glad you think this shit is funny." I shook my head and drank some more henny from the bottle in my hand.

I drank Hennessy so much that it tasted like water, but if I drank enough it would still make me numb to feeling. That's what I needed to feel right now. Nothing.

"I mean it's good to know that the Tin man got a heart,

but we at a strip club right now and there's ass everywhere so I'm going to need you to stop acting like a bitch and let's fuck this club up like old times." He got up and smiled at me before jumping on the stage.

He walked up to the stripper that was sliding down the pole and whispered something in her ear before pointing at me. She smiled at him and then grabbed the money out of his hand putting it in her bra. She walked seductively off of the stage and down to where I was sitting. She wrapped her arms around me and smiled in my face. I couldn't lie she was fine as fuck and her body was on point, but for some reason I wasn't feeling her like that. She continued to grind in my lap just looking at me.

"How about you shake that ass or something and stop grinding in my lap like it's ameture night." I snarled in her face as I drank some more henny.

She looked at me for a second before rolling her eyes and turning around. She was definitely shaking everything she had as I downed the bottle of henny I was drinking. I was getting tired of her so I pushed her out of the way and stood up making my way to the bar.

"Aye let me get a bottle of Henny." I signaled the bartender not caring if he was serving anybody.

He quickly came over and placed the bottle on the counter and I put a hundred dollars on the counter. I walked away from the bar, but not before cracking open the seal on the bottle. I drank the dark liquid with my eyes closed as I walked back to where Mitch was sitting getting a lap dance from the girl I had pushed off of me.

I chuckled and was about to sit down in the seat next to him when I was tackled to the ground out of nowhere. It seemed like the whole club stopped. The music turned off and the lights were on now. I looked up to see four police officers around me pointing their guns at me plus the one on my back.

"Pharaoh Rivera you are under arrest for the kidnapping of Cameron Michaelson." The officer on my back spoke before picking me up off the floor.

"Damn y'all *pendejos* couldn't have waited until a nigga was done with his bottle." I slurred talking in third person.

"It seems like you've had enough. You have the right to remain silent. Anything you say can and will be used against you in a court of law. You have the right to an attorney. If you cannot afford an attorney, one will be provided for you. Do you understand the rights I have just read to you?"

"Yeah man let's get up out of here so I can call my lawyer." I sucked my teeth and then quickly looked back at Mitch nodding my head.

He knew exactly what he needed to do.

———

"$\mathcal{F}$or the last time I don't know shit and I don't know who y'all even talking about. Can I go now? Damn do I have to say it in Spanish?" I questioned looking at the detectives.

"We need you to answer a couple of questions. We have witnesses who place you at the scene."

"Scene? What scene? What are y'all even talking about right now?" I questioned like I was confused.

Just then the door to the interrogation room opened and in walked the person who I had been waiting on all night.

"Pharaoh doesn't say anything else. Come with me." Mya spoke walking up to me, grabbing a hold of my shoulder.

"What are you doing here? He can't leave." One of the detectives spoke.

"I'm Mr. Rivera's lawyer and you two have no proof, no witness, and nobody tying my client to these claims that y'all are trying to pin on him. We will be leaving now and if you two need to get in contact with my client anytime after this you are to come to me. He will not speak to anyone without me being present. If you two pull another stunt like this again I will have your badges. Now Mr. Rivera, get up and let's go." She stated sternly looking directly at me.

I quickly stood up and followed her out of the room. I was surprised to see her talk like that, and it turned me on. I couldn't help but look at her ass and how tight her slacks fit her. When we made it to the car I noticed Mitch sitting in the driver seat. I walked over to the passenger side door and opened it for Mya before getting in the backseat.

Once we were all in, Mitch drove out of the parking lot and down the street. It was silent for a while until Mitch spoke up.

"I handle that problem for you Ro." He spoke quickly looking at me through the rear view mirror.

I knew exactly what he was talking about so I just nodded my head. I knew that letting Rebecca go without killing her would lead her to go talk to the police so I talked to a couple of people who knew her. I got her full name, work address and house address. I waited until she snitched and then I gave Mitch the word. The police couldn't prove I did anything if they didn't have bodies or witnesses.

"So y'all two really about to sit here and talk in code like I'm not here?" Mya asked, looking between me and Mitch.

I sat quiet for a second in thought. It wasn't that I couldn't trust her. I just didn't think she would take what I do for a living the right way. She was going to have to find out eventually.

"This is attorney client privilege. Whatever we say in this car doesn't leave this car. It's best that I know what's going on so when questions start getting asked I will already have a story. Here hand me both of your phones." She held her hand out for our phones and we passed them to her.

She turned both of them off plus hers and then put them all in the glove compartment.

"One of y'all better start talking." She crossed her arms on her chest and laid back on the door so she could see both of us.

"It all started when I met Ro at the play area in preschool." Mitch started talking, making me laugh and shake my head.

"Nigga she not talking about how we met you dumb fuck." I continued to laugh making them both laugh along with me.

"I'm not playing. Tell me what's going on." She said seriously, calming her laughter.

"Alright basically I run everything from the West end to the Grove with Mitch. Us and the niggas from the Valley don't get along and that's what I want to run. They did drive by's in my territory and I retaliated leaving dead bodies everytime. Now a couple months ago when I got locked up for them drugs being in my car, I found out that one of my boys got set up. When I got out I got the names of everybody who was involved. Damien and Tyrone were the ones who set it up. Tyrone came looking to see if you knew anything about the money because Damien didn't give him his cut. I found out that Damien gave it to his babymama Camille. I shot her tosend Tyrone a message. Once Tyrone is gone I'll be able to control the valley. I'm hoping that Tyrone takes the bait and comes to the meet up I set up with Camille Sunday night." I told her looking her in the eyes so she knew I wasn't lying.

"It all makes sense now, but I just got one question. When Tyrone met me at my office he had no idea where Damien was, and then I remembered what Aaliyah and Kris told me before I met him. If Damien had died in the hospital from the car accident why did the doctors say he checked himself out and where is his body? You seem good at disposing bodies, so where did you dispose of his body Pharaoh?" She asked the question of the year catching me off guard.

I looked at her for a minute just thinking of how I should tell her.

"Chloe and Chaos had him for dinner the night of the accident. When I left for a couple hours and came back." I told her honestly.

The look of disbelief came across her face and then disappeared as quickly as it came.

I knew it took a lot for Pharaoh to tell me what was going on, so I forgave him a little bit but I was still mad at the fact that he permanently injured Camille for revenge. That wasn't going to stop me from being there for him though. I couldn't let my kid grow up and have to go see their dad in jail. I was going to do everything in my power to keep him out of jail.

"So you didn't tell us what happened the other day when Pharaoh got arrested." Jessica said, taking a sip of her wine as she continued painting.

Kris, Aaliyah, Jessica and I were at a paint and sip event to hang out and talk while we got our creativity on. I was able to sip any wine so I sipped in orange juice in a wine glass so I wouldn't feel left out.

"They basically tried to charge him with kidnapping but

they couldn't produce the witness who told them in the first place and with no body or evidence they had to let him go." I stated simply shrugging my shoulders.

"You think he did it?" Aaliyah asked.

"At this point I don't know."

"So y'all not together anymore because you don't like his lifestyle?" Kris asked confused.

"No he did some things that I wasn't okay with."

"At least he told you hoe. I think anything is better than you getting your ass kicked everyday over nothing." He stated referring to Damien.

"I'm with Kris on this one. So what if Pharaoh doesn't do what normal men do when it comes to making money. He perfected his skill and he makes a lot of money doing what he has always known how to do. You shouldn't knock him for that. He really loves you Mya and he would never intentionally do anything to hurt you." Aaliyah added.

"To me he is this sweet and sensitive person, but to everybody else he's a monster and it scares me like what happens when he gets mad at me? Who knows what he is capable of." I exclaimed looking at them.

"See that's your problem, you are trying to compare him to Damien. Damien is dead and he's not coming back to hurt you. Pharaoh made sure of that. Why would he do that if he was just going to start beating your head in too?" Kris questioned taking a sip of his wine.

"I don't know Kris." I rolled my eyes.

"Exactly so you should go talk to him."

"I'll do it tomorrow, he is busy tonight." I explained.

Tonight was the night that he went to get his money back from Camille so I was hoping everything was going good.

"How are you ladies doing tonight?" Came from the side of the table.

We all looked over to see Tyrone standing smiling down at us. I was confused as to what he was doing here and not on his way to the meet up with Camille.

"Who is this fine piece of chocolate?" Kris asked, taking a sip of his wine.

"One of my clients. What are you doing here?" I questioned, confused.

"Let me talk to you outside for a second." He smiled ignoring my question.

He waited for me to get up and then we walked outside together. Once we made it outside I was about to turn around and ask him what he was doing here again, when I felt something pressed against my back.

"Don't scream and don't try to run." Tyrone spoke against my ear.

I would have been more scared if he wasn't so fine and he smelled so good.

"Why are you doing this?" I questioned.

"Just walk, we are going for a ride." He answered ignoring my question again.

I walked with his gun pressed to my back until he told me to stop and tossed me a set of keys. They were the keys to an all black mustang.

"You are driving, and let me get your phone." He held his hand out as he opened the driver side door for me.

"You know if you wanted me to go somewhere with you, you could have just asked me." I rolled my eyes and handed him the phone, getting into the car.

"It ain't even about that right now. I have other plans for us baby girl." He closed the door and then walked around and got in.

He clicked around in my phone before smiling and putting the phone to my ear. He must have put it in speaker because I heard it ringing.

"You can start driving." He demanded looking over at me as the phone continued to ring.

"You didn't even tell me where we are going."

"Just drive." He stated before the phone stopped ringing.

"*Bebita?* What's up is everything okay?" I heard Pharaoh's concerned voice come through the phone and I looked over at Tyrone in disbelief.

Tyrone smiled at me before putting the gun to the side of my head and signaling me to be quiet.

"She is good for now, where are you at?" Tyrone answered.

"Who the fuck is this and why do you have Mya's phone." I could hear the anger building up in his voice.

"Calm down she's driving to come meet you, and I didn't want her talking on the phone and driving since she got a gun to her temple and a baby in her belly. Where are you at though?" Tyrone questioned unbothered by the tone in Pharaoh's voice.

"If you hurt her I swear to god I'll kill you." Pharaoh sneered.

"Just tell me where you are so we can meet up and handle it." He chuckled not caring about what Pharaoh was talking about.

"I'm at the courts in the grove." Pharaoh gave in and told him.

"Bet we will be there in ten minutes." Tyrone said before hanging up the phone and sticking it in his pocket.

He told me to make a left and then turned the radio on as we headed to meet up with Pharaoh.

———

*W*hen we pulled into the parking lot of the basketball courts I saw Pharaoh and Mitch sitting on top of Pharaoh's car. We got closer and by the looks on their faces they were pissed. I parked the car and looked over at Tyrone to see what he wanted me to do next.

"Get out and walk over to my side of the car. If you run over to them I will empty this clip into your back." He snarled.

"If you shoot me then they will kill you." I explained.

"You and that baby you carrying will still be dead so it would be worth it. Now let's go." He rushed me.

I didn't understand what the men in California problem was. They were too damn fine to be so evil and filled with hatred. I rolled my eyes and then got out of the car to let him out. This was exactly what I was talking about when I said I didn't want to be involved. Too bad I was already deep into it.

Tyrone got out of the car and instantly got behind me putting the gun to my back. He told me to start walking and I walked until I got a couple feet from Pharaoh. They both slid off the car with their gun drawn.

"¡Let her go *pendejo!*" Pharaoh yelled out, aiming his gun at us.

"Ro you know I can't do that." Tyrone chuckled.

I was really getting tired of him.

"She ain't got shit to do what we got going on." Mitch added.

"She got just as much to do with it as Camille and DJ. Aye Ro is this really yo baby in her stomach or is it Damien's? I guess she likes switching sides too." Tyrone sneered.

It felt like his lips were close to my ear.

"She doesn't switch sides like you. You a opp" Mitch interjected.

"Opp? Nigga yo head was so far up Pharaoh's ass to see that he wanted to control everything. He treated me like shit. In the Valley they treated me like I was family."

I was so clueless until those words came out of his mouth. Tyrone was doing all of this because he wanted to get back at Pharaoh. If you ask me the whole reason behind it was stupid and pointless. I wish I was back at the sip and paint with my girls, but I guess Tyrone needed me because if he hadn't come here with leverage against Pharaoh he would be dead by the time he stepped out of the car.

"You just as dumb as Cameron. You have to work to be at the top my nigga. Ain't nobody gonna just hand shit to you. That's why them Valley niggas broke and most of them dead. All of them except you." For the first time tonight I saw a sinister look come across Pharaoh's face.

I could feel the barrel of the gun on my back shaking. I knew Tyrone was scared because I was scared for him.

"Mya I need you to be still." Pharaoh stated looking me dead in my eyes.

Just as he said that he let off a shot and I became stiff as a board. A bullet flew past my ear and Tyrone went limp and fell to the ground. When I turned around Pharaoh had hit him dead between the eyes.

I quickly ran over to Pharaoh and hugged him tight, he smiled and hugged me back before pulling away.

"You did good, you okay?" He questioned as he looked me over for bruising or cuts.

"Yes I'm okay he didn't hurt me." I responded nodding my head.

Just as I finished my sentence about four or five police cars pulled into the parking lot and turned the lights and sirens on surrounding the three of us.

This just got a whole lot worse.

Chapter Twenty-Four

PHARAOH

"Fuck! What do they want?" I yelled out in irritation.

This was the wrong time for the police to show up.

"Drop your weapons and get down on the ground with your hands behind your head." One of the police officers warned us.

I looked back at Mitch and nodded my head as I dropped the gun and kicked it out in front of me before I slowly raised my hands in the air. I got on my knees and then slowly laid on the ground but I never took my eyes off of Mya.

Once the officers made sure that me and Mitch were down they rushed us. They ran right past Mya like she wasn't even standing there. They quickly surrounded me like they were fighting to see who got the arrest first.

"I'm down and I have no weapons on me. Some of y'all go

make sure my girl and our baby are straight. It doesn't take this many people to arrest me." I argued as my face was being used to clean the concrete because of all the people on top of me.

Once I was cuffed some of them went to check on Mya and then I was picked up off the ground. I made eye contact with Mya and saw that she was crying.

"Let me say goodbye to my family." I begged as I watched the tears fall from Mya's eyes.

"Alright let's go. You got one minute." One of the police officers holding me said.

We walked over to where Mya was standing and she wrapped her arms around me.

"*Mira me Mira me (look at me)*. Don't you get soft on me Mya, you are going to be good. We are going to be good. Just fill Jessica in on what's happening and go home to get some sleep. I'll be in touch with you in a little bit. *Te amo*." I smiled and placed my forehead on hers since I couldn't touch her.

She kissed my lips and held onto my face before letting go. I looked at her one last time before they pulled me away. They put me and Mitch in separate cars and then we were driven away from the scene.

Once we got to the police station they put me and Mitch in separate rooms across from each other. They told me we were arrested for shooting Camille and kidnapping Cameron. I knew meeting up with Camille wouldn't end well so when they made me go through line up and I knew exactly who was on the other side of the glass. They would come talk to us one after the other and every time they did they were getting nothing out of us. Then they put us in the same room and to try and make us talk.

Mitch and I sat in silence just thinking silently together.

"Ay you get up out of here and you go and tell them I got something they want to hear." Mitch stated finally looking at me.

"What are you talking about *Mano.*" I asked, shaking my head.

I knew exactly what he was getting ready to say but I didn't want him to.

"You know exactly what I'm talking about. Before we got pulled into the bullshit together what did we promise each other?" Mitch questioned making me look at him. "What did we say?"

"If we were to get caught up together and it was no other way out, one of us was going to box up the Jordan's. Who ever had less to care for." I repeated our oath.

"You got Mya and your kid to look after, ya mom and pops. Even down to yo damn dogs man. They need you out here fam on some real shit. Ain't nobody really out here for me except you and Trey. Who is going to get bad hoes from the West end to the Valley? Nigga this is perfect timing. Everybody scared and they running around not knowing what to do next. You have to go and handle it, let them know how you handle business." Mitch used our secret language just in case somebody was listening.

He was right though. I was going to push dope from the

West end to the Valley and all I had to do was let the Valley niggas know how I ran my business.

"What are you going to do *Mano*?" I asked, still concerned.

"Nigga I'm going to kick my feet up and chill out for a while. Watch you from the inside. I'll want to go outside again one day." He smiled and held his hand out and waited for me to give in. "I'm going to be straight most of my family up in here, don't worry about me. Just make sure I ain't gotta worry about not eating and you visit every once in a while to keep me posted and shit." He held his hand out further and I chuckled and shook his hand.

"I owe you one." I spoke standing up.

"Yeah I know you do, go ahead and tell them I'm ready to talk before I change my mind." He chuckled before I knocked on the door letting them know her they could come back in.

Once they got Mitch's confession I was free to go. I had to make sure that Mitch served no time in jail. I owed him that. He kept his word to me and I would forever be in debt to him.

———

*W*hen I finally made it home it was three o'clock in the morning. Right now I needed to be up under Mya and I knew she needed me.

"Mya? *Bebita!*" I rushed upstairs to our room surprised to see her laying in bed crying her eyes out.

Beside her lay Chloe and Chaos, and Chloe was the one scooting Mya the box of tissues and letting Mya lay on her like a pillow. Chaos was at Mya's feet trying to go to sleep. When he noticed me standing in the doorway he quickly got up and walked out of the room. I chuckled and looked at Mya who stared at me in disbelief.

"Pharaoh did you- they let you out?" She questioned sitting up on the bed.

"How about I tell you what's going on in the morning right now I just want to take all your pain and fears away. I want to only think about you right now. I walked up to the bed and saw Chloe looking at me.

"Chloe, I can handle this, you can go in your room." I told her.

She looked at me for a second and then looked at Mya for reassurance.

"I'm okay Chloe you can go to bed now." Mya rubbed her belly for a second and Chloe wagged her tail.

Then she stopped and jumped off of the bed slowly making her way out of the room. Not once did she take her eye off of me until she got completely out of the room. I looked at the opened door in disbelief for a second before closing the door and looking at Mya.

"She finally loves me." Mya spoke joyfully.

"I see that." I shook my head as I took off my shirt and tossed it to the side, walking up to the bed.

"You've been through a lot tonight. Why are you still up?"

I questioned sitting on the bed next to her and rubbed her belly.

"I was worried about you." She explained dropping her head.

"Well I'm here now." I lifted her up a little and kissed her stomach.

She smelled immaculate so I continued to place kisses down her stomach. She ran her hands through my curls begging me to go lower and I did exactly what she wanted. I pulled her boy shorts down along with her panties and feasted in her forbidden fruits. If Eve's pussy tasted like this Adam would have eaten her instead of the apple.

I went in on Mya's pussy there wasn't anything nobody could say or do to stop me at this point. It was game over. I wasn't going to give her the dick tonight. I was giving her just enough to work her up and tire her out.

After she came and I drank her juices I stood up and started taking my pants off. She thought we were about to go for a ride, but I had other plans. I've been playing ball at the courts all day and then I decided to lay in the dirt for the police. I needed a hot shower ASAP.

"Where are you going?" She asked as I walked over to the bathroom.

"I'm about to take a shower. You should be getting to sleep." I smirked knowing she wasn't feeling it.

"How are you going to just start something and not finish?" She asked, confused.

"I'm good. Go to sleep, we can talk about it in the morning." I chuckled and walked into the bathroom and closed the door.

Even though I wanted so bad to get in between Mya's legs, I wasn't even clean. Plus there was a lot of frustration I had built up and I needed to be by myself tonight. She will just have to wait until tomorrow morning, so I wouldn't take my frustration out on her.

Chapter Twenty-Five
MYA-2 MONTHS LATER

I paced the hall, my palms were sweaty and I felt like I was walking on broken glass. I've always hated coming here, but I had to if it helped in the long run. I closed my eyes and took a deep breath before I heard my name being called.

"Nyomi hey? Are you okay? I kinda lost you there for a minute." Jessica asked, bringing me out of my thoughts.

"Yeah yeah sorry I was just thinking. You know how I get when I'm in here." I confessed.

"Everything is going to be okay. This is just the three of us going to visit him for a minute to let him know what's going on. He's been in here for two months just sitting and waiting. We will be in and out." She informed me before placing her electronics in the box.

"Come on he's waiting for us." She smiled and grabbed my

hand, before walking to the double doors that led to the visitation room.

We walked in and my eyes instantly landed on Pharaoh. He smiled at me and stood up. We had been waiting for ten minutes before I walked out to wait for Jessica.

"You feel better *bebita?*" He asked concerned once we were close enough.

"Yes I'm okay." I nodded my head.

"Okay good, they went back to get him. He should be coming out in a minute. How are you doing Jessica?" Pharaoh asked, smiling up at her.

"I'm okay, when are they bringing him out?" She questioned sitting down at the table.

"He should be out in a minute." Pharaoh grabbed my hand and sat down making me sit down with him.

This was Pharaoh could talk about for the past two months and it was adorable. He was like a kid waiting to see Santa on Christmas Eve. I couldn't blame him though because him and Micah were joined at the hip, so him not being able to speak and talk to him for two months was a lot to ask for.

A couple of minutes later we heard a door opened and in walked Mitch with two armed guards at his sides. When he saw the three of us his eyes lit up for a split second before they turned cold.

He sat down at the table and the guards were still on each side of him looking straight ahead.

"I'm cuffed and shackled ain't nobody going nowhere, can

y'all give us some space." He spat at the both of them causing them to mean mug him and walked away from the table.

"Damn aren't y'all a sight for sore eyes." Mitch smiled and looked between the three of us.

"What's up man, how are you hanging here?" Pharaoh questioned.

"Man it ain't shit like my home but it's cool man. What are they talking about on the outside?" He asked before he crossed his arms on the table.

"I'm trying to get the trail to be set at an early date then what is it right now, but they want it held eight months from now. They only want that because all their leads have dried up and none of the witnesses are willing to step forward. They lost their only lead to the Cameron case and they are trying to find Camille so that they can have a witness to her case, but she is M.I.A." Jessica started off.

"Why do I have to stay in here until then? What about bail or something." Mitch asked, confused.

"See that's the problem, you had an open warrant for a minor drug charge so the judge declined our request for bail because you were also caught with a loaded gun that wasn't registered. A 9mm. The same type of gun that was used to shoot Camille in her leg." I answered smirking at him trying to get him to catch on to what I was saying.

The only people who knew that both Mitch and Pharaoh had the same gun were Pharaoh, Mitch and I. Yes they were the same gun but they weren't going to be able to match the shell casings. The real gun was giving back to Pharaoh, who got rid of it a long time ago.

"Okay and what's that supposed to mean?" He asked, still confused.

"They have to match the shell casings if they don't you are free to go." I smiled and he looked around the table.

He had finally understood what I was saying.

"How long does it take them to do that?" He questioned.

"Shouldn't be too much longer *mano(Brother)* . You'll be home in no time." Pharaoh stated nodding his head.

"Cool cool, well thanks for the news let me get back in here. I get to school these niggas on the courts in a minute." Mitch stood up and then chucked up the deuces, before turning around and walking to up to the guards.

Once he was through the doors we all went our separate ways. I was glad Pharaoh and Mitch worked with me because even though they took this oath to each other, the only way they could be charged with murder is if the shell casings match. If one of them chose to go to jail for the other, they didn't have to stay in there long.

———

"*D*o we really have to wait until the baby is born to know it's sex?" Pharaoh asked for the umpteenth time since I told him I wanted to wait.

"Yes we do, that's the whole point of waiting to find out." I chuckled and laid down on his chest.

We were laying in the house watching tv. Today was one of the few days where I had Pharaoh all to myself and I was going to take advantage of that. We were still working through our differences, so I still haven't moved back with him. I need to know that I'm not ever put in harm's way again.

"What about the baby shower how are people going to know what to buy?" He continued.

"We can tell them to buy everything in unisex. Nothing pink or blue. We can make the colors be red, green, and white. You know the color of the Mexican flag. To embrace your roots. Plus it gives me and my friends a chance to taste some authentic Mexican cuisine." I answered running my hands down his torso.

"My mom cooks a lot of Mexican food. Old family recipes from *mi gran abuelas (my grandparents)*. You're going to love it." He smiled and flicked my nose.

"That sounds promising."

"It does, doesn't it?"

"Yeah I can't wait until him or her comes. Four months in and five more to go." I did my little happy dance making him laugh.

"All of that is cool, but when are you going to be mine again? I'm tired of only getting to see you twice a week. It's getting closer to the baby being born and I want you here, at home permanently. I need you here with me not going back and forth from here to the loft." He explained.

"I told you I needed time Pharaoh?" I lied.

"Time for what? We are good, we communicate well. You know everything about me and we are having a kid soon. I'm not just saying that to try to control you or get you to be with me again. I just want you to come home. You need to be here. I don't want you to have to go through this alone and by yourself ever." He saw right through my lie and all I could do was drop my head.

One side of me feels safe and secure when it comes to Pharaoh, but the other side is scared because I don't know what happens when he's angry.

"I'm scared Pharaoh." I finally confessed.

"Scared? Scared of what?" He looked at me and I looked at him.

When he figured out what I was talking about he looked disappointed and dropped his head.

"Why are you scared of me Mya? What about me scares you?" He asked in disbelief.

"You're anger. What will happen if I make you mad." I stated.

He laughed for a second before looking at me for a second and dropping his head again.

"Damn, he really did a number on you *bebita*. What do you want me to do Mya? My mother always told me "*Una reina debe ser adorada. Todos sus deseos deberían cumplirse. Ella debe ser protegida y nunca debería ser lastimada por su rey.*" That means a queen should always be worshipped. Her every desire should be met. She is to be protected and she should never be harmed by her king. Mya that was the main rule in my family. No man should ever lay hands on a female for any reason. Mya I love you and no matter how mad I get or how bad my day is, I will never lay my hands on you. I promise you that. I'll kill myself before I ever think about putting my hands on you." He stuck his pinky out and looked up at me.

"What's that for?" I questioned, confused.

"Promise me right now that we can start over. The past is the past. We leave everything that has happened in the past and we start over."

I looked at him with a straight face for a while before giving in and intertwining my pinkie with his. He finally smiled and I knew he was relieved.

"We can start over." I smiled while our pinkies were still intertwined.

"Alright. So uh, hey I'm Pharaoh. Could have sworn I saw you before. Can I get your name?" He smiled and held his now free hand out for me to shake.

"I'm Mya." I played along and shook his hand

"That's a beautiful name. How far along are you?" He asked, pointing to my bump.

"Thank you and almost five months." I chuckled.

"Is the father in the picture if you don't mind me asking?" He reached over and started rubbing my belly.

"He is actually. One of the most amazing people this world has to offer." I smiled and he looked up at me and I could have sworn his eyes twinkled.

"Swear? Damn he must be one of the luckiest men in the

world. So you sure we haven't met before?" He questioned cracking a smile.

"You mine again now stop playing and come give me some." I whined, not wanting to play anymore.

This whole thing turned me on and now I needed some dick. He laughed and shook his head before crawling between my legs.

"*Te amo bebita (I love you babe)*." He looked me in my eyes and he made me wet.

I loved it when he spoke Spanish.

"*Yo te quiero más (I love you more)*." I responded pulling him closer until our lips touched.

Chapter Twenty-Six

PHARAOH-2 MONTHS LATER

"*H*old on, so you walked in and what happened Ro?" Mitch snickered across from me at the visiting table.

I had been coming here to visit him every other Friday since they allowed him visitors. I made sure he had enough money on his books so he didn't have to worry about needing anything. I made him feel comfortable and the people we had on the inside kept him safe. I even went the extra mile and got him a conjugal visit with Aaliyah. He was happy I surprised him for the first time. I told him I was going to visit but instead I let Aaliyah go since they both kept bothering me about seeing each other. Why not kill two birds with one stone. I'm letting them see each other and take care of my *Mano* while he locked down for the moment.

"Basically the first thing I do when I walk in is ask for

whoever was in charge. I guess they went to get him and when I tell you they came back with the skinniest and weakest nigga they could find. Man this nigga was corny as fuck. He really thought he was gangsta though. Had his stick all out walking up to me and shit. I'm like are y'all serious right now. So he walked up to me and was like why is there a Grove nigga in my trap." I stopped and looked at Mitch.

He looked at me with a straight face for two seconds before we both started laughing. It was a good thing I was allowed private visits since I was the only family Mitch had. We would have been told to be quiet by now.

"Come on man," he started laughing and then calmed himself down. "Then what happened?" He asked like he already knew where the story was going.

"I stood just looking at him and he got mad and went to pull his stick on me." I laughed and shook my head because Mitch had been laughing before I could get my sentence out.

"You smoked him didn't you?" He couldn't stop laughing so he could only get a few words out at a time.

"I know everybody is going to try some shit with me so I didn't really care about that. This nigga had the audacity to point the gun at me sideways."

"You hit him with the special didn't you." He was laughing so hard that he was crying.

"I just pieced him up and grabbed the gun out of his hand. Then I pointed it at him and shot him between his eyes. He had to die."

It was disrespectful how he came at me. Anybody who

would cross me now will cross me later on in life and I didn't need them in my way.

"Damn nigga how are you going to kill the lil nigga with his own gun?" Mitch shook his head trying to keep himself from laughing.

"I had to because of the way he held the gun up at me."

"Wow! So now you got the Valley on lock?" He questioned.

"Not yet. Once you get out you can run it however you want. The Valley is yours. I just got them out running petty errands right now so that I can snuff out the snakes. That should be taken care of by the time you get out.

"You for real right now?" Mitch asked in disbelief.

"I'm deadass serious. It's all yours *mano*." I nodded my head.

"*Es por eso tú es mi perro (that is why you my dog)*." He smiled and held his hand out for a handshake.

"*Entonces hablamos español ahora(so we speaking spanish now)?*" I questioned

"Un pequeño (a little) but for real thank you for everything man. You're like the brother I never had. I wouldn't be here today if it wasn't for you."

"*No es nada (It is nothing)*. You my brother. If you shoot, I'm shooting first." I smiled and waved him off.

"Last thing before I go. I need one more favor though."

"What's up *mano?*"

"I think Aaliyah is pregnant. I won't know for sure until

next week, but if she is. Can you watch out for her until I get out?" He asked, throwing me off guard.

"Uh...yeah man I got you and if I don't you know Mya will." I chuckled.

I was happy for Mitch even though I would have never thought he was the one who would ever settle down.

"Alright imma get up with you later and tell MaMa I said what up." He called Mya by the nickname he gave her. He stood up and chucked the deuces before turning around and walking to the door.

He knocked on the door twice and stepped back so that the door didn't hit him when it opened. A couple seconds later a guard opened the door letting Mitch through. I sat there by myself for a couple of minutes and then I got up and walked to the door knocking again.

"*H*ey Doc I just stopped by on the way home to ask you a couple of questions if you got some time." I walked up next to Mya's doctor hoping we could speak for a second.

"I have a couple minutes left on my break. Come on walk with me to my office." He answered looking back at me briefly as I followed him.

Once we got in his office I sat down in the chair in front of his desk and waited for him to sit down.

"To whom do I owe this visit to?" He asked curiously as he sat down in his chair. "Is Nyomi doing well?"

Dr. Fulton was a middle aged white name who delivered thousands of baby's. I knew that because Mya made me look through a bunch of different doctors until we found him. She wanted our baby to be born healthy with no complications.

"Yeah she's okay. I know we were here a couple days ago to check on the baby and I know that you know the sex of my baby. So can you tell me if I'm having a girl or a boy?" I questioned hoping he would tell me.

"Mr. Rivera I'm sorry but Mya told me not to tell you or her the sex of your baby until he or she is born." He stated sympathetically.

"I got a hundred thousand for you right now if you tell me." I reached into my pocket and pulled out the stack of money and put it on his desk in front of him.

His eyes widened at the sight, but then they went back to normal.

"Mr. Rivera I can't take your money and I can't tell you what the sex of the baby either, but I can tell that he or she is a very healthy baby." He smiled and leaned back in his chair.

"Alright you don't have to tell me. Just let me see the ultrasound pictures. I can figure it out by myself." I suggested not taking no for an answer.

I slid the money to him and smiled before he shook his head and scooted his chair back to his filing desk. He opened one of the drawers and combed through some of the files until he found the one he was looking for. He picked it up and scooted backed to his desk, sitting the manilla folder in front of me. I quickly grabbed it and opened it. It was all the paperwork on Nyomi and the baby. I looked through it until I found what I was looking for. Four little pieces of paper that were paper clipped together. I took the paperclip off and studied the pictures. I had no idea what I was looking at until I got to the last one.

I smiled and looked at the paper closer. My heart melted when I realized what I was looking at.

"*Voy a tener una hija!* I mean I'm going to have a daughter." I repeated myself so that the doctor understood.

Every time I said daughter it shocked me. I was bringing a little angel into this world soon and she was going to grow up knowing that I'm always going to be there when she needed me.

"Congratulations Mr. Rivera. I don't have to worry about Mya finding out about any of this do I?"

"No no," I wasn't worried about Mya finding out about time knowing the sex if he baby, but there was something that I still needed to know for sure. "One more thing Doc. How fast can you do a DNA test?" I questioned.

"You don't think this baby is yours?" He asked, taken back.

"I mean yeah but in the beginning of her pregnancy Mya was with someone else and I just wanted to make sure the baby is mine." I answered honestly.

It wouldn't matter to me if the baby wasn't mine. I just wanted that satisfaction of knowing she was a hundred percent mine.

"Well you feel strongly about this and you got a little time on your hands, so we can get your DNA and I can have it sent to the lab for testing today." He agreed to do the test.

"I got some time for this." I handed him back the manilla folder and stood up.

I pray to god she turned out to be mine.

Chapter Twenty-Seven

PHARAOH-3 WEEKS LATER

"*L*et's get straight to business. You give me what I came here for. I got two hundred grand for it and we can go about our day." I spoke straight up not wasting no time.

I was at home chilling with Mya when I got a call saying that somebody named Enrique had some cocaína he wanted to show me. I told him to get it together and I'd be on my way. Now I was standing in front of him hopefully he had what I drove over for. It was a long drive out of my way and I didn't feel like killing anybody today.

"Show me the money first and then I will go get your bricks." He stood there like he was unbothered by me.

"I don't make purchases until I make sure this is legit. I have your money right here," I tapped the duffel bag on my shoulder. "Now show me what I came here for before I get mad."

He looked at me for a couple of seconds and saw that I wasn't playing around before turning around. He walked over to a table which had a duffel bag on it and opened taking one out. He then walked over to me and handed it to me.

"Aye Shane come here and let me see your knife." I yelled out to one of the niggas I came here with.

Shane walked over to me and handed me the knife. I cut it open and dug some out with the knife before putting it to my nose to test it out. I only sniff cocaína to test it out. I knew what was going to sell and I knew what was going to flop.

"Alright I'll take it." I handed Shane back the knife and took the duffel bag off my shoulders and tossed it on the floor in front of him.

Instead of picking up the bag first like I thought he would, he walked back over to the table where the *cocaína* was and brought it over to me.

"It's fifteen bricks in there just like we talked about." Enrique stated handing the bag to me.

"It's all good. Hit me up if you come up with anything else." I grabbed the bag and put it on my shoulder.

I made sure everybody I had come with was around before I walked out of the building and to my car.

"Aye Shane put this in your car and take it to the warehouse. Make sure they cut it up and get it out there ASAP." I tossed him the duffel bag and opened the door to my car.

"On it boss." Shane caught the bag and then chucked the deuces before walking to his car.

I nodded my head and got in the car before driving off.

———

"Okay Mya got your BBQ wings and chili cheese fries and Aaliyah I got your philly cheese steak, extra cheese no green peppers." I spoke as I walked into the living room and handed the girls their food.

Since we found out that Aaliyah was pregnant, I have been taking care of her and Mya. I went to all of her appointments just like I did with Mya. She still slept at her own house but during the day she was with me and Mya. It was cool even though that meant Kris wouldn't be too far behind.

"Hold on so they get food and I don't? I'm here to nigga?" Kris shouted out before I could even hand the ladies their food.

"Chill out! Let me get them their food and then we can talk about you eating." I shouted out, tossing him the bag with my burger and fries in it.

I wasn't that hungry anyway.

"Okay chico you don't have to throw shit." He whined back, getting me upset.

"Shut the fuck up and get you funky ass feet off my glass table," I yelled out before calming myself down. "Y'all enjoy y'all food I'm going upstairs to take a shower." I sucked my teeth and mean mugged Kris one more time before walking up the stairs to my room.

Stripping out of my clothes and putting my phone on the bed I walked into the connected bathroom. I turned the water on steaming hot and stepped into the shower.

When I got out of the shower I put on clothes and then walked downstairs to see what was going on. I walked into the living to see Kris dancing around. I sighed and walked around the couch so that I could sit next to Mya.

"What is he doing?" I questioned sitting down and pulling Mya onto my lap.

"Being Kris. How'd everything go with Enrique?" She asked, kissing my cheek.

"It was cool. I got what I went for. Are you feeling okay?" I questioned checking up on her.

"Yes I'm okay, and thank you for the food. I'll make sure I make you something to eat since you gave yours to Kris." She chuckled.

"I should have told him to go get his own damn food." I sucked my teeth still mad about giving my food to him.

"I thought you were going to." She laughed.

"I thought about it, but I didn't feel like hearing his voice. You know how he gets it."

"Yeah you're right. I love you baby." She leaned in and kissed me.

"I love you more bebita." I kissed her back.

My phone started ringing so I dug it out of my pocket to see that it was the hospital calling. Hopefully the doctor had the results for my DNA test. It had been on my mind ever since I walked into his office three weeks ago. I thought Mya was going to find out a while ago, but she had no idea. I needed it to stay like that.

I tapped her leg letting her know to get up, and she slid off of me. I then answered the phone and stood up making my way to the kitchen.

Once I was out of earshot, I put the phone to my ear.

"What's up doc?" I questioned as I walked around the Island counter.

"Hey Mr. Rivera, sorry about calling so late in the day, but I was calling because the DNA test results came in today." He spoke through the phone.

"Alright well let me hear it then." I smiled excitedly as I continued to pace the kitchen.

"Okay let's get right to it. From what it says here Mr. Rivera your DNA is a ninety-nine point nine percent match to the baby that Mya is carrying." He stated.

I stood there and smiled as I pieced together what he had just said.

"I'm the father?" I asked in disbelief.

"Yes, at least that's what it says right here."

"Thank you Doc. You go ahead and you have a good night." I smiled and hung up the phone before putting it in my pocket.

"I'm really the father." I said out loud to myself.

"Yeah and I thought we made that known when I found

out I was pregnant." Came from behind me making me stop what I was doing and turn around.

Mya was standing at the opening of the kitchen with her hands on her belly. She was starting to cry and I quickly walked up to her, but she held her hand up stopping me in my tracks.

"I thought we said we weren't going to keep secrets from each other Pharaoh. Then you go behind my back and get a DNA test without telling me? What's up with that?" She asked through her tears.

"I needed to know for sure, it had nothing to do with you." I tried to explain.

"So why didn't you tell me? You went behind my back when you could've just told me. What else have you done that you are not telling me?" She questioned.

I wanted to tell her that I found out the sex of the baby but that would just make it worst.

"That's the only thing." I lied.

"If that was the truth, why did the doctor give me this?" She pulled a stack of money out of her pocket and tossed it on the counter.

I knew instantly that the money on the counter was money I had given the doctor to tell me the sex of the baby.

"That's-." I was about to try to explain myself, but she put her hand up and stopped me again.

"Until you can learn how to tell me the whole truth, don't talk to me." With that she walked away leaving me in the kitchen looking stupid.